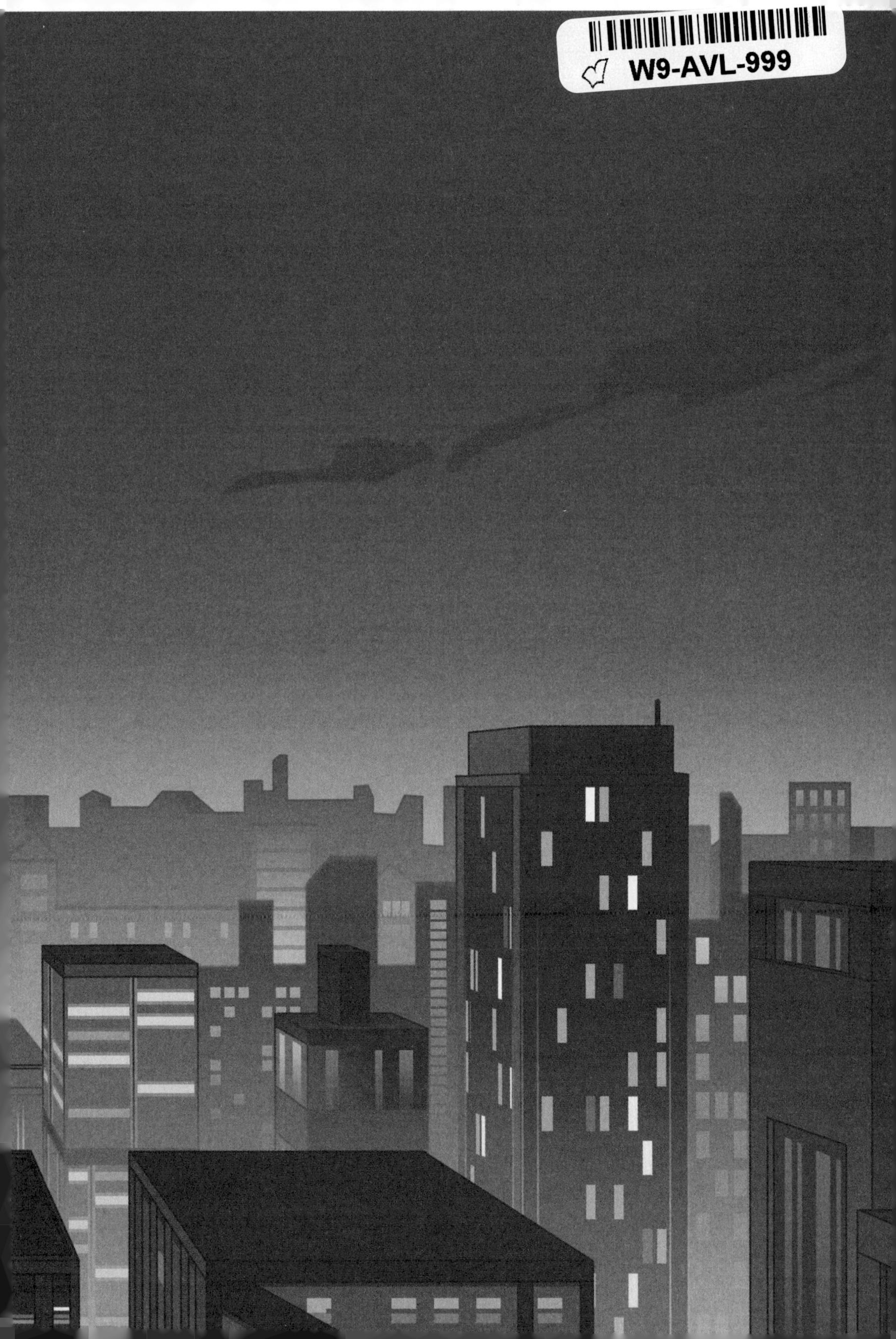

Library of Congress Cataloging-in-Publication Data
Names: Hitchcock, Laura, author. | Melaranci, Elisabetta, illustrator. |
Priori, Giulia, illustrator.
Title: Catch that crook! / by Laura Hitchcock ; illustrated by Elisabetta Melaranci
and Giulia Priori.
Description: New York : Random House, [2018] | Series: DC Super Friends |
Series: Beginner books
Identifiers: LCCN 2018005173 | ISBN 978-0-525-64600-6 (hardback) |
ISBN 978-0-525-64602-0 (lib. bdg.) | ISBN 978-0-525-64601-3 (ebook)
Subjects: | BISAC: JUVENILE FICTION / Media Tie-In. | JUVENILE FICTION /
Comics & Graphic Novels / Superheroes. | JUVENILE FICTION / Action & Adventure /
General.
Classification: LCC PZ7.H629555 Cat 2018 | DDC [E]—dc23

Printed in the United States of America
10 9 8 7 6 5 4 3 2 1
First Edition

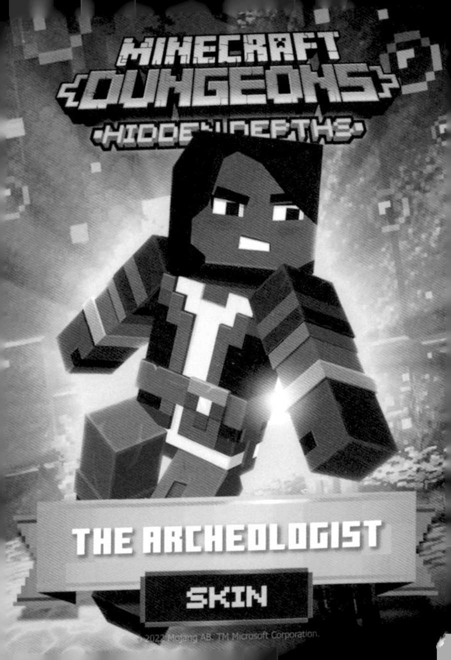
MINECRAFT
DUNGEONS
HIDDEN DEPTHS
THE ARCHEOLOGIST
SKIN

THE ARCHEOLOGIST

SERIES 2

#85/98 RARE

This isn't just any archeologist. This is THE Archeologist. If it's got bones, they know all about it!

WWW.MINECRAFT.NET

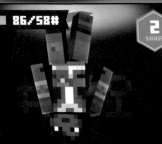

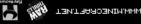

CATCH
THAT
CROOK!

By Laura Hitchcock

Illustrated by Elisabetta Melaranci and Giulia Priori

BEGINNER BOOKS®

Random House 🏠 New York

Batman is a super hero.
He keeps Gotham City safe!
Robin is Batman's sidekick.

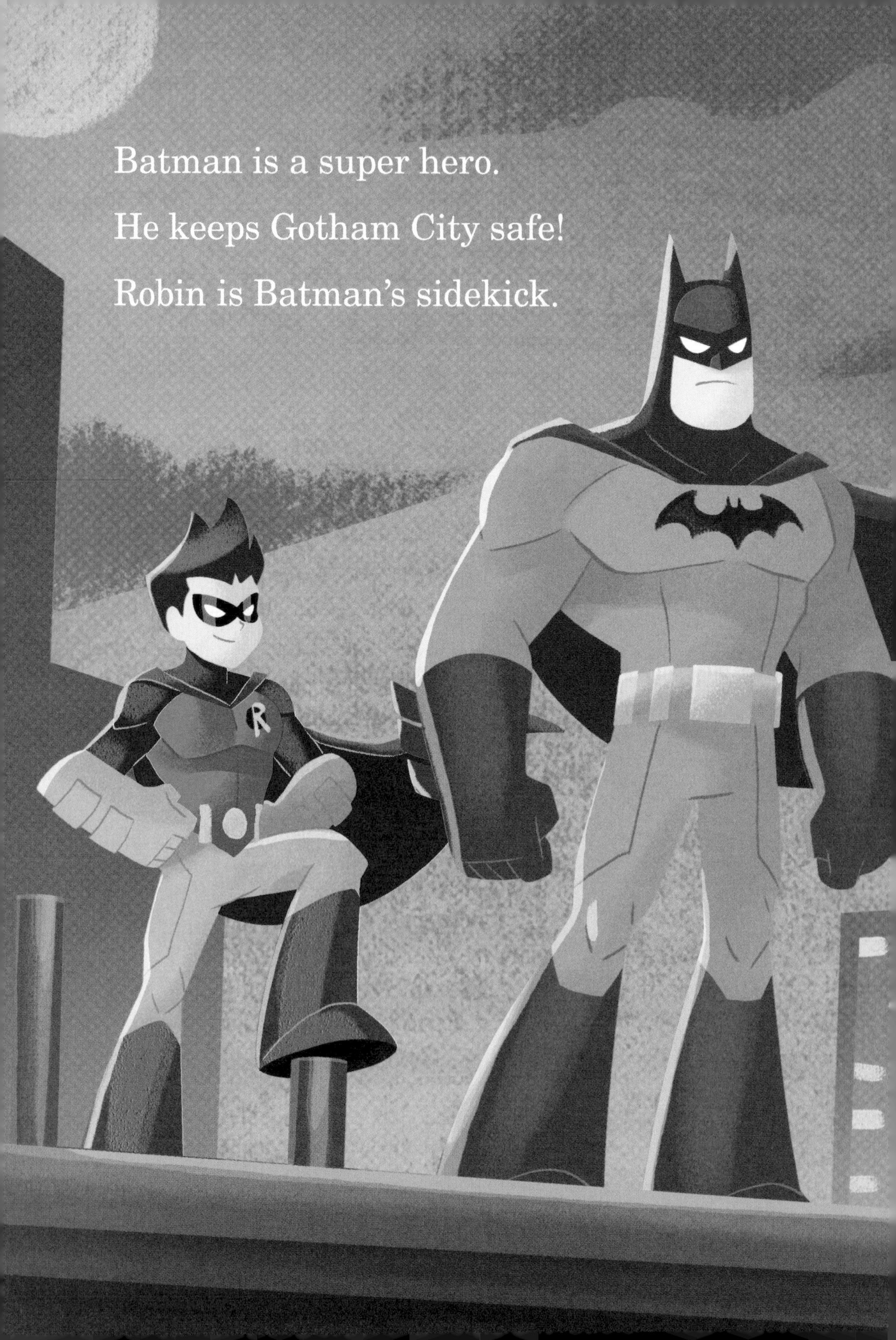

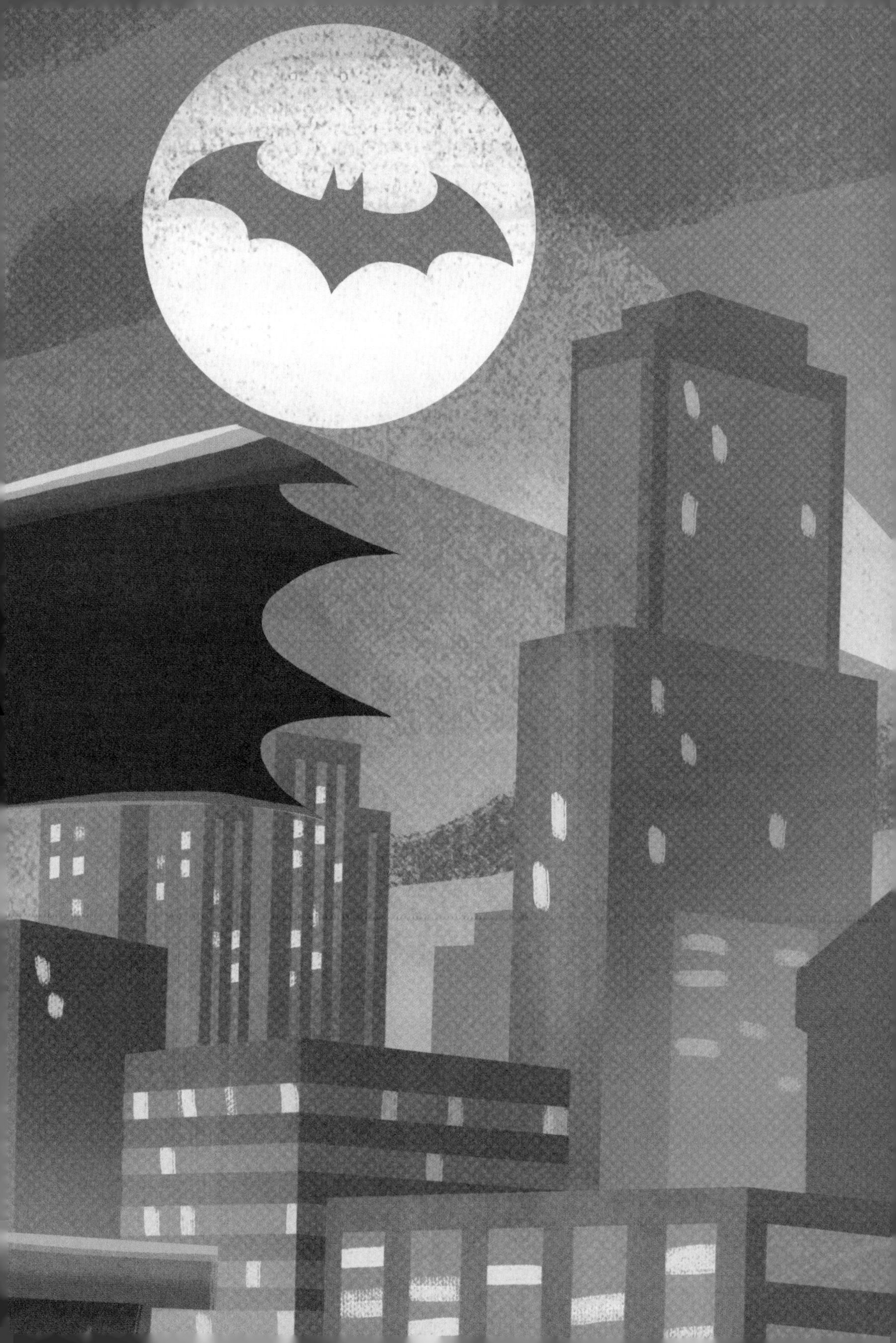

Batman checks the computer.

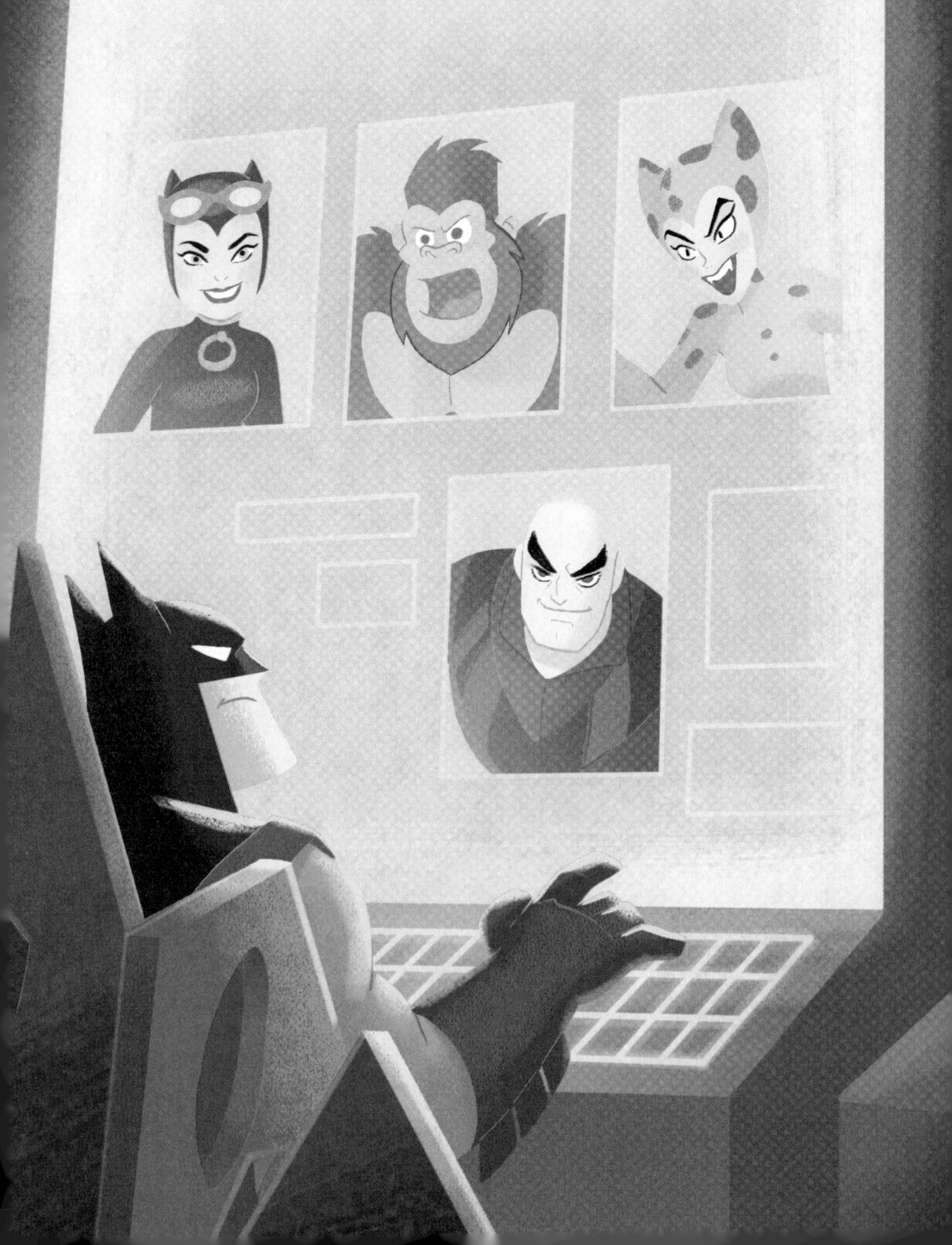

Robin works in the lab.

Every night, Batman gets ready.

He puts on his gloves.

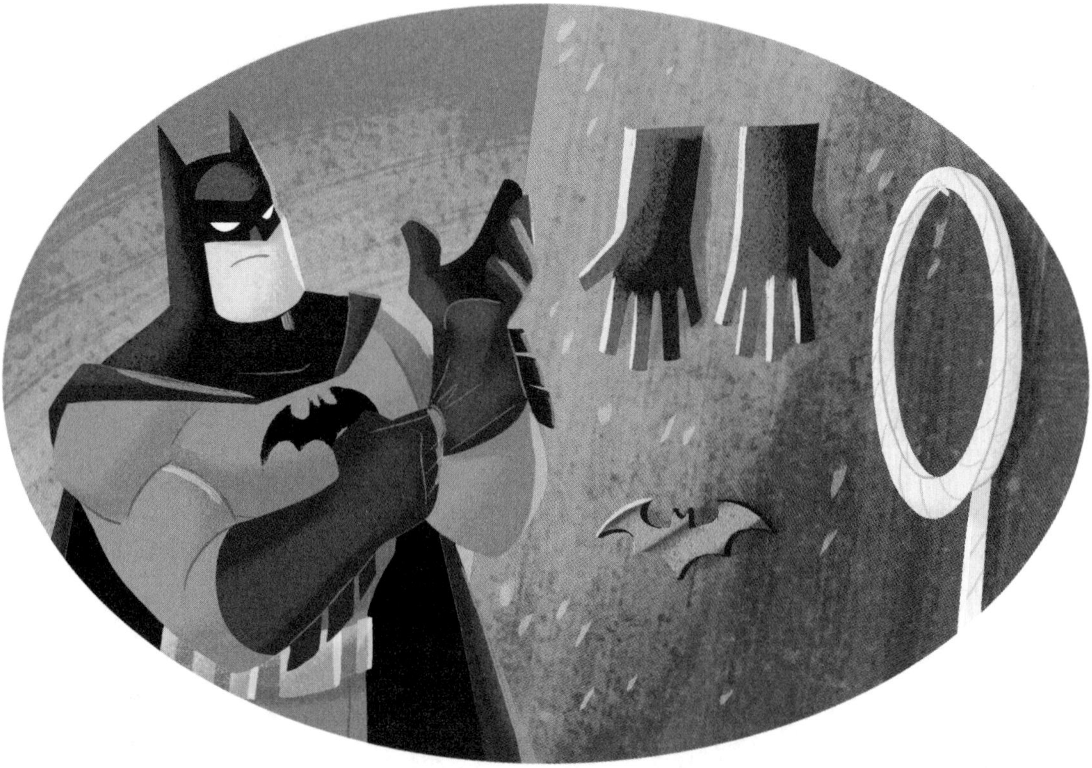

He checks his Utility Belt.

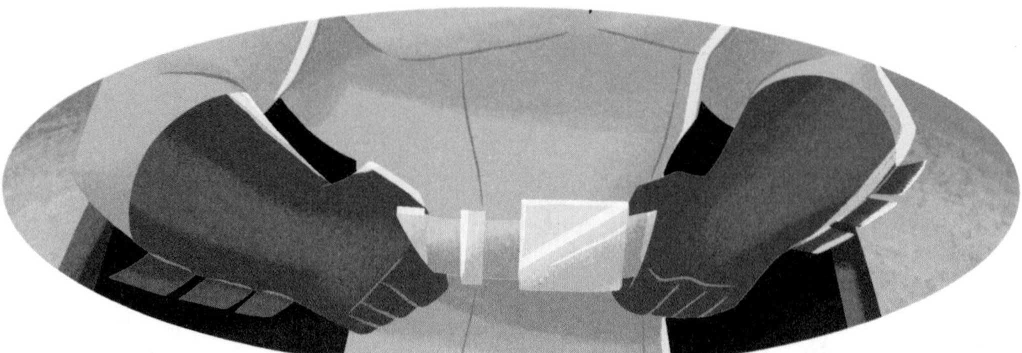

Uh-oh!

Robin sees the Bat-Signal

in the sky!

Someone needs their help!

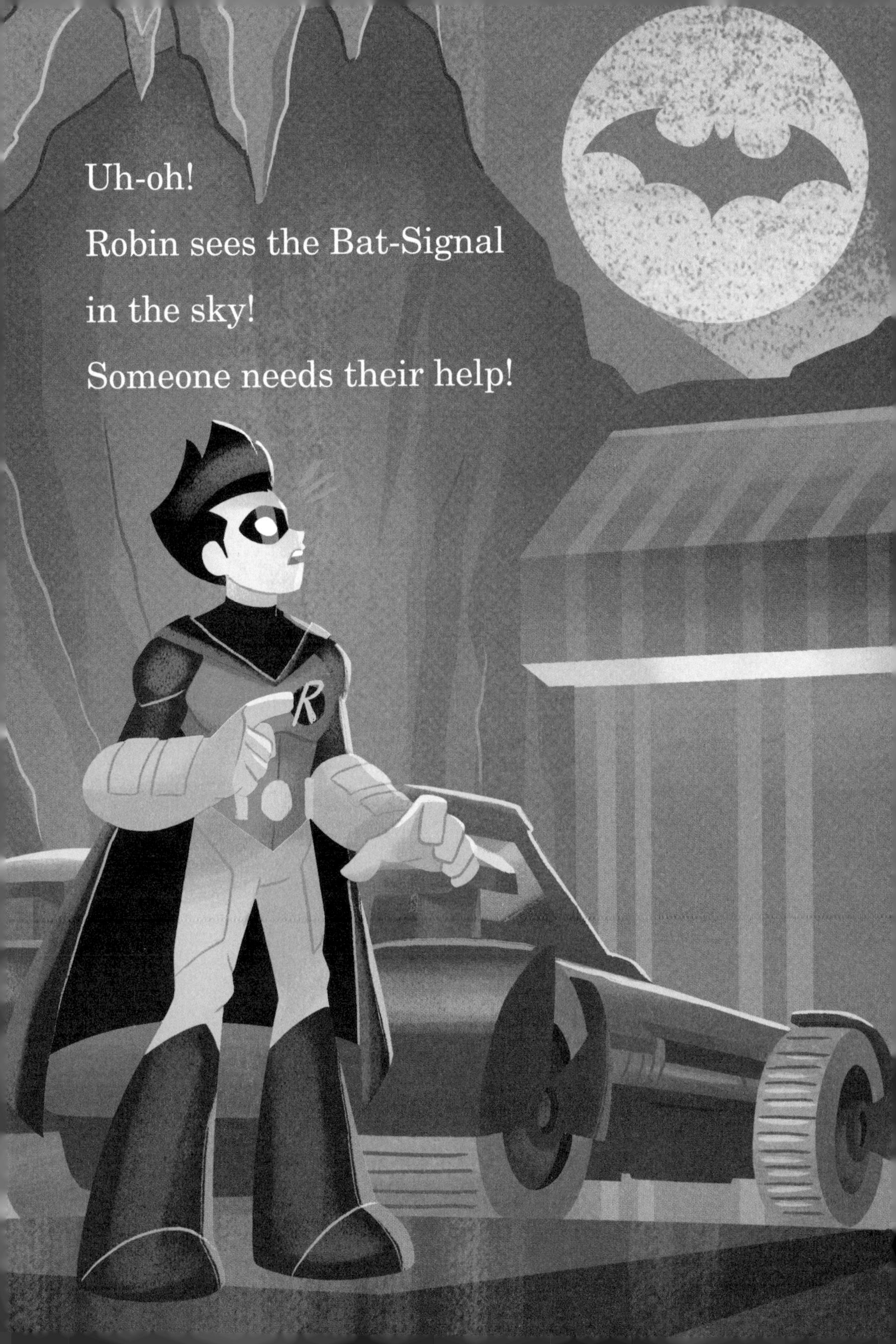

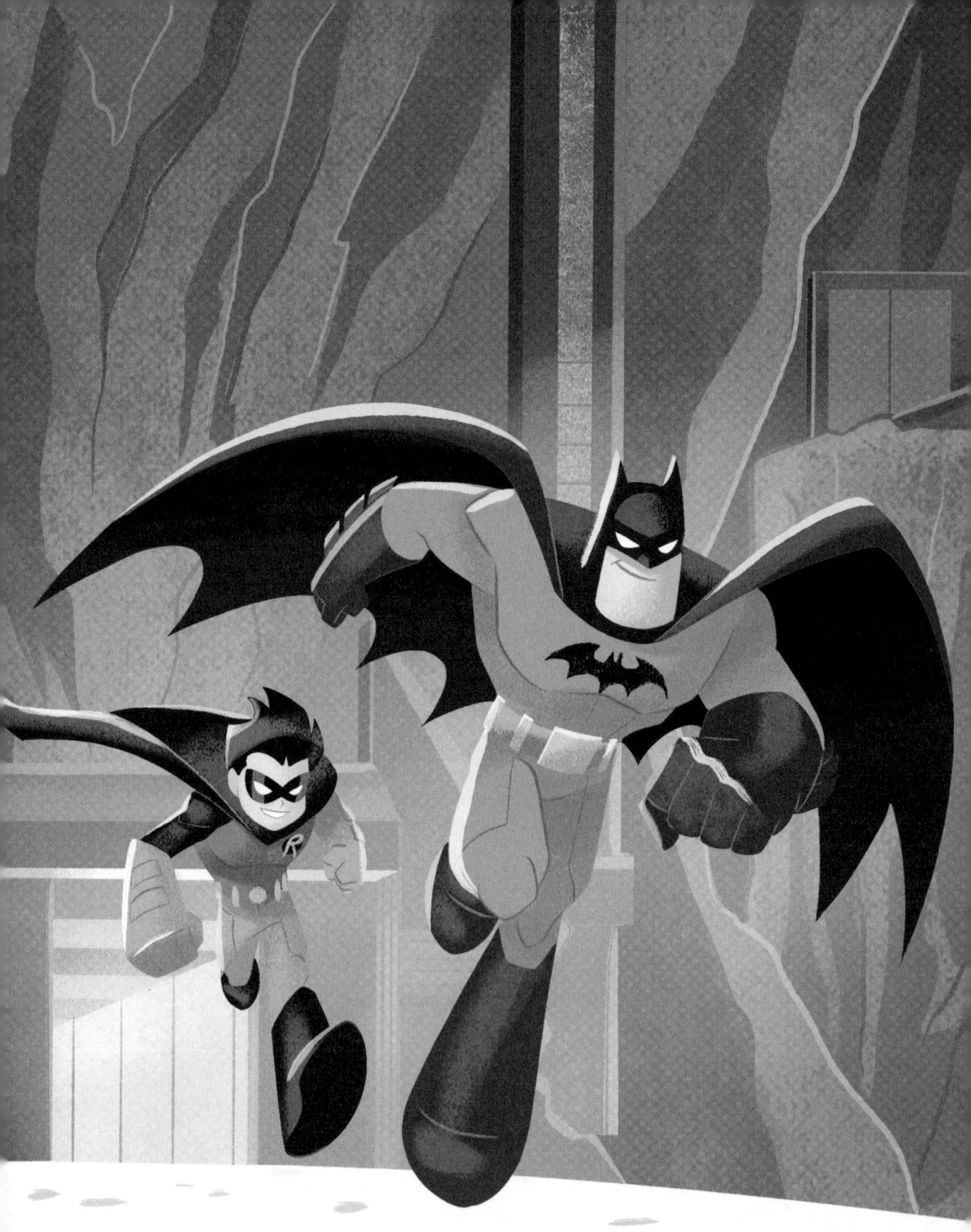

Batman and Robin are ready to go!

The heroes jump
into the Batmobile.
They must go to Gotham City.
What will they find?

At the police station,
they learn that
someone is robbing the bank!

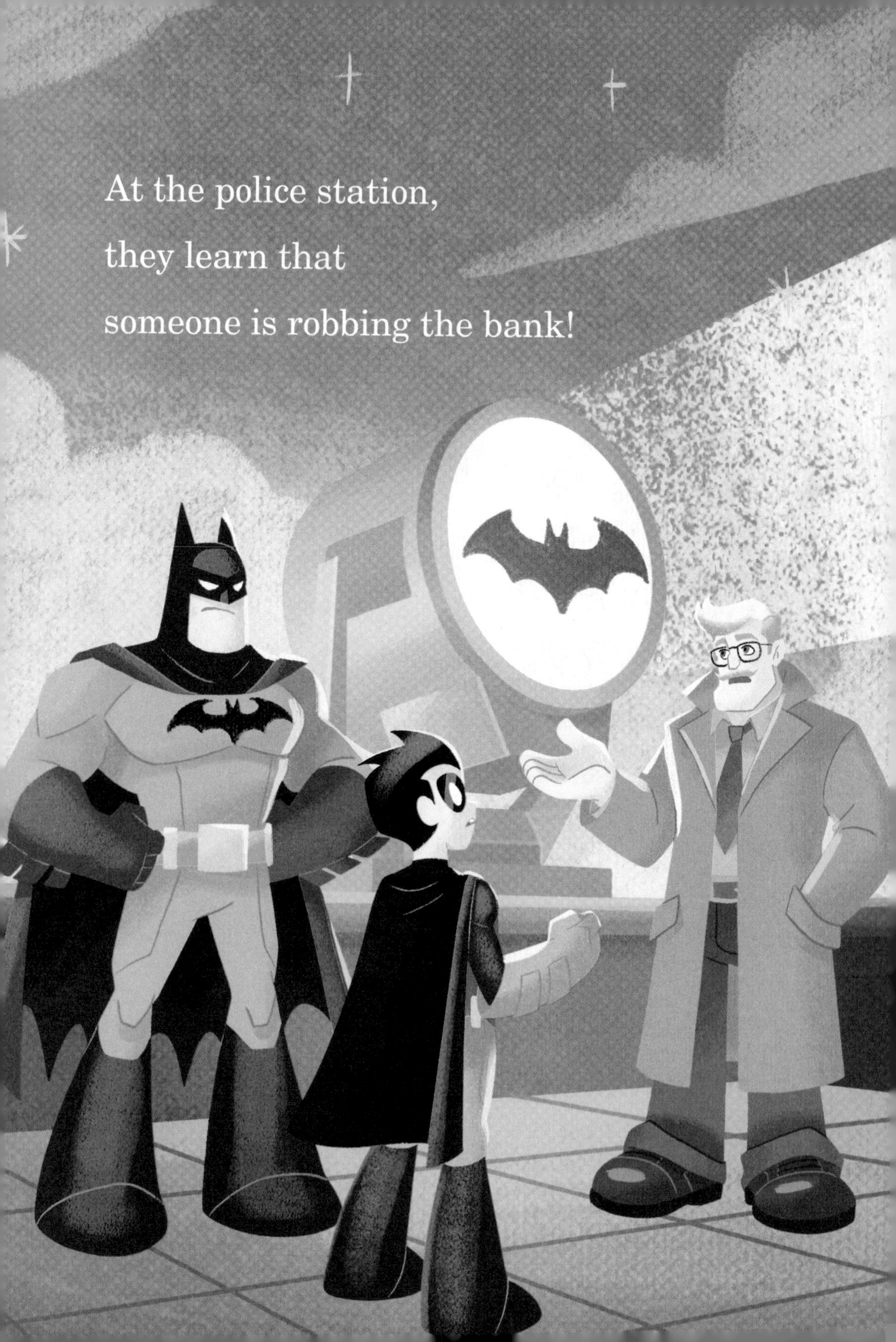

The heroes race to the bank
in the Batmobile.

The street is dark.

The bank is quiet.

Where is the crook?

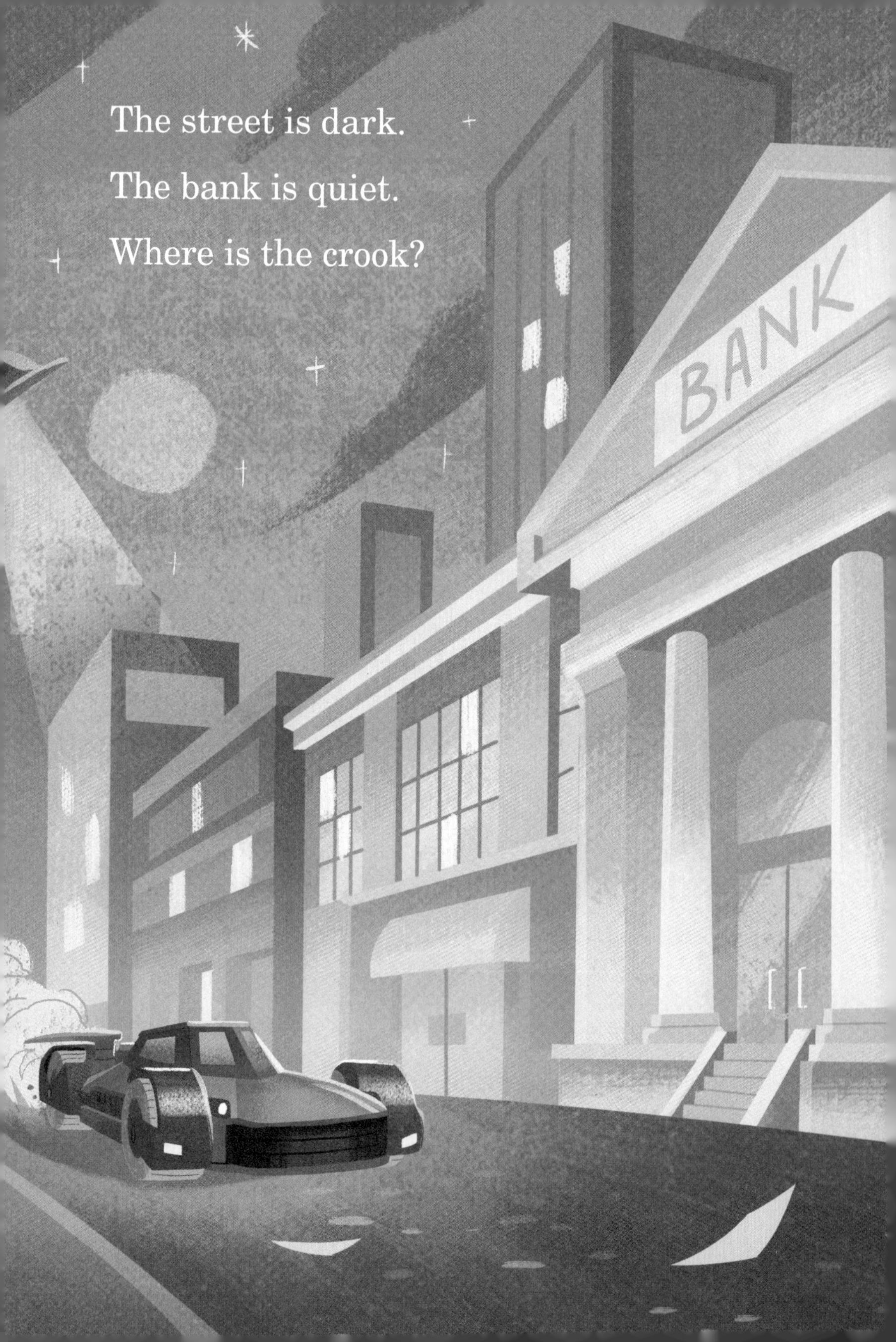
BANK

Robin sees a clue—a broken lock!

Batman spots Catwoman.

She is in the bank!

“Let’s catch that crook!” says Batman.

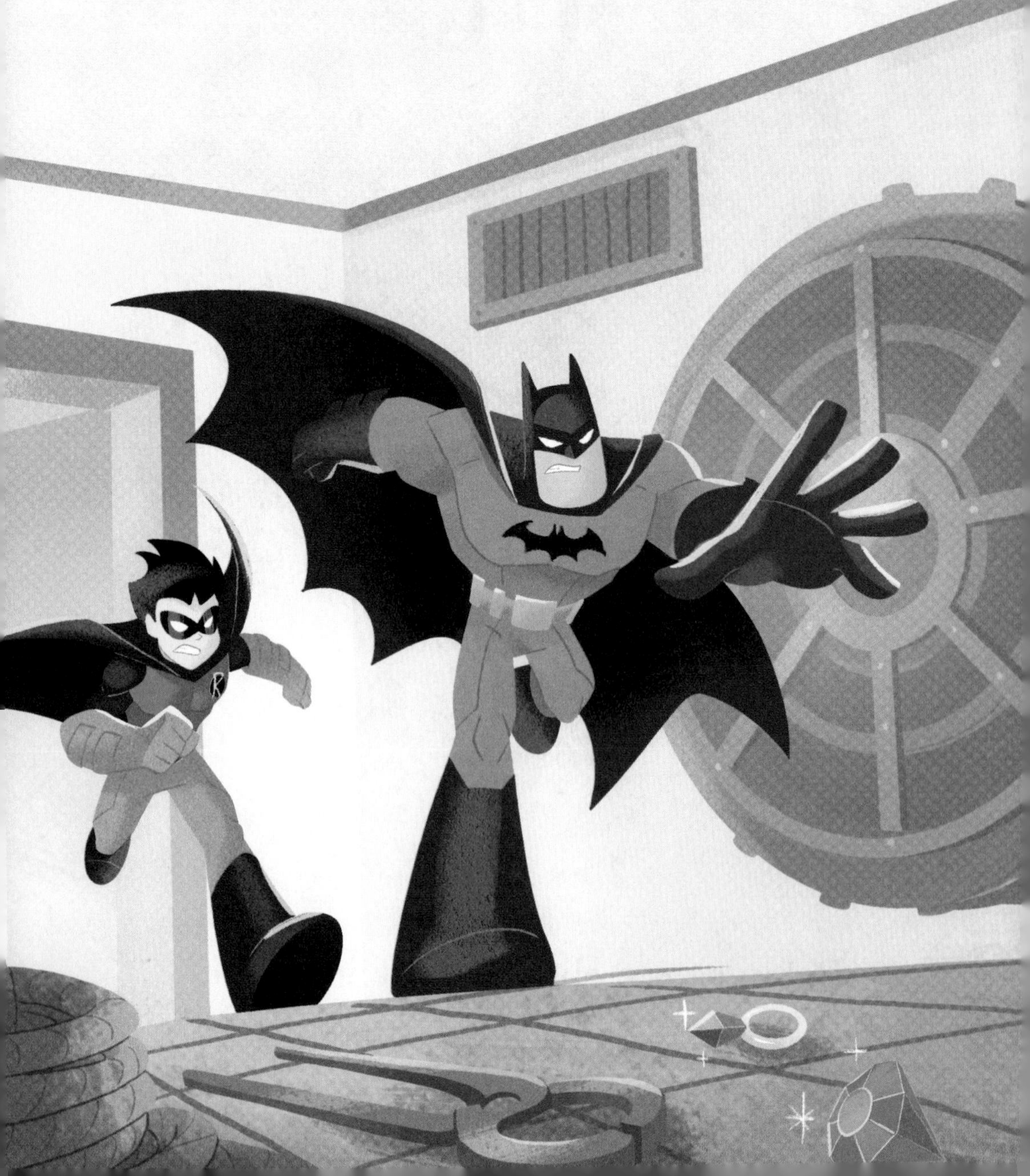

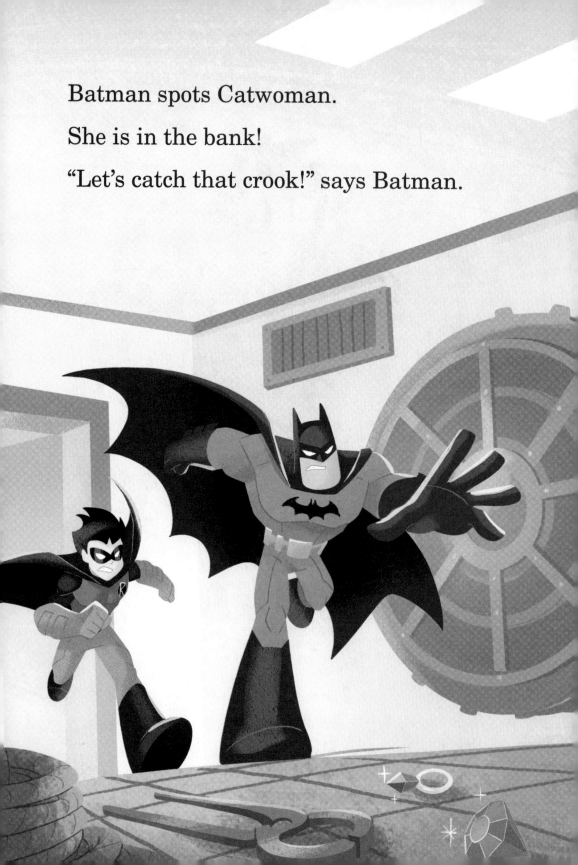

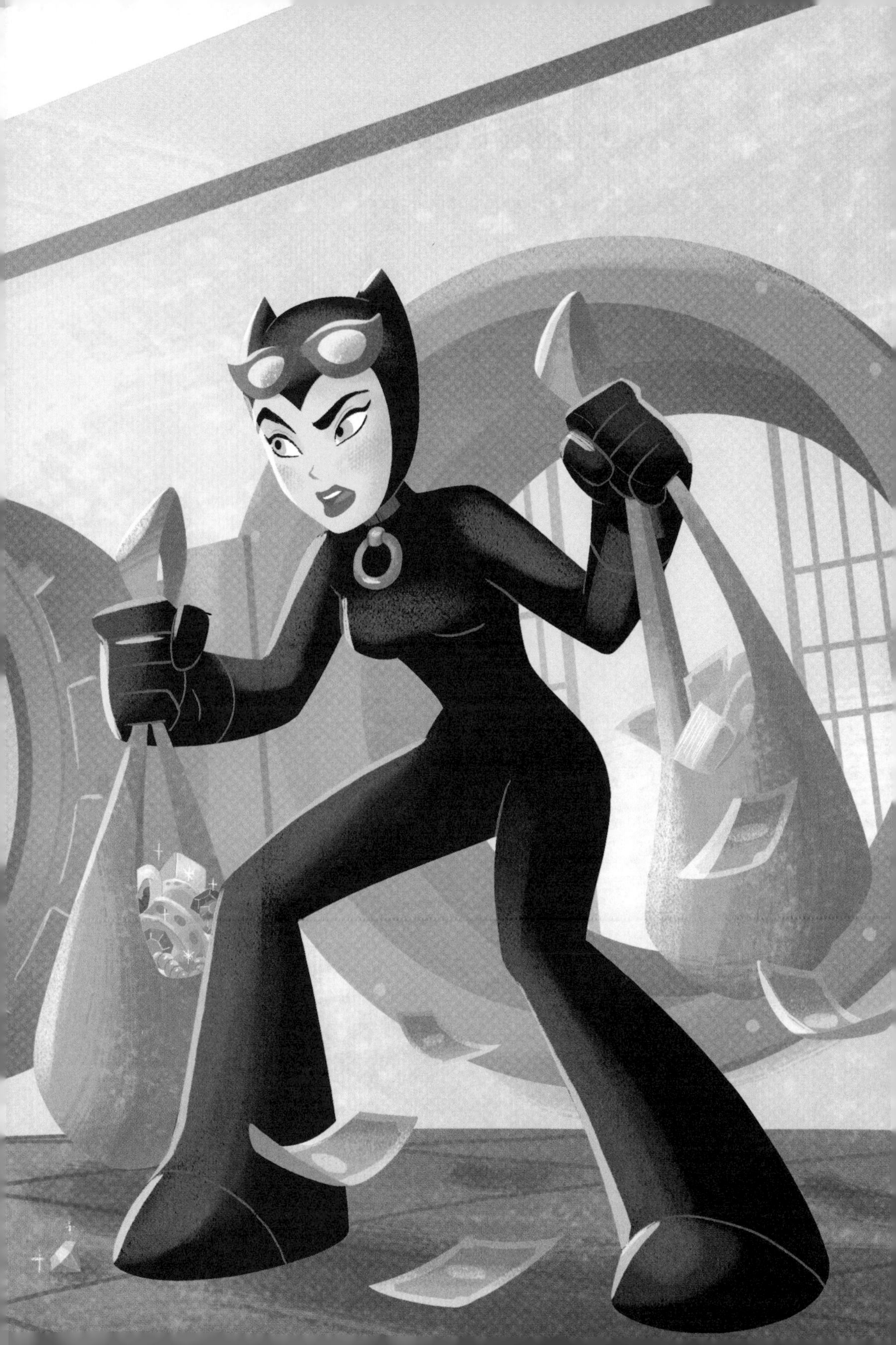

Catwoman tries to get away.

Batman chases her!

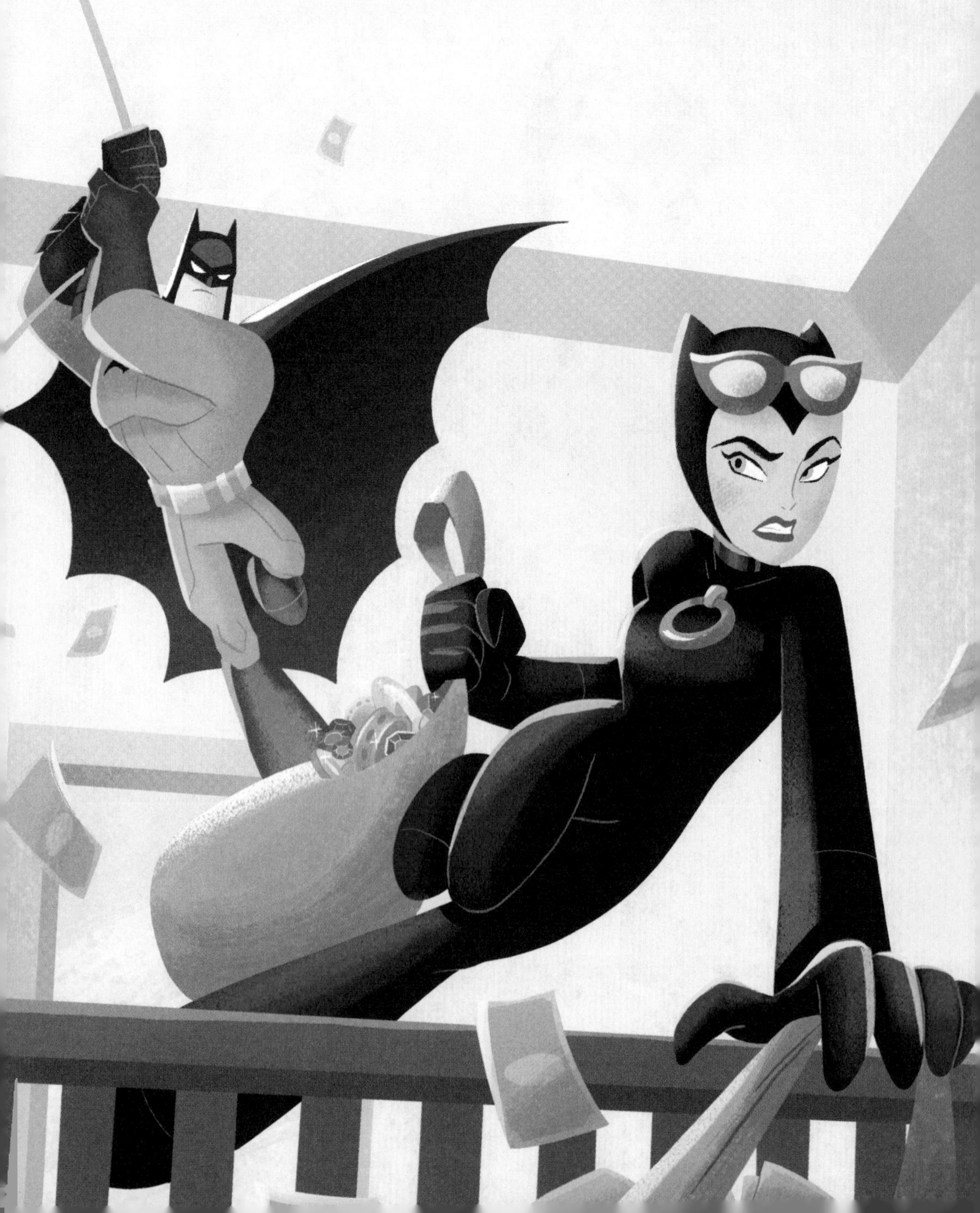

Batman throws his Batrope.

He catches the crook!

Then the heroes hear an alarm.

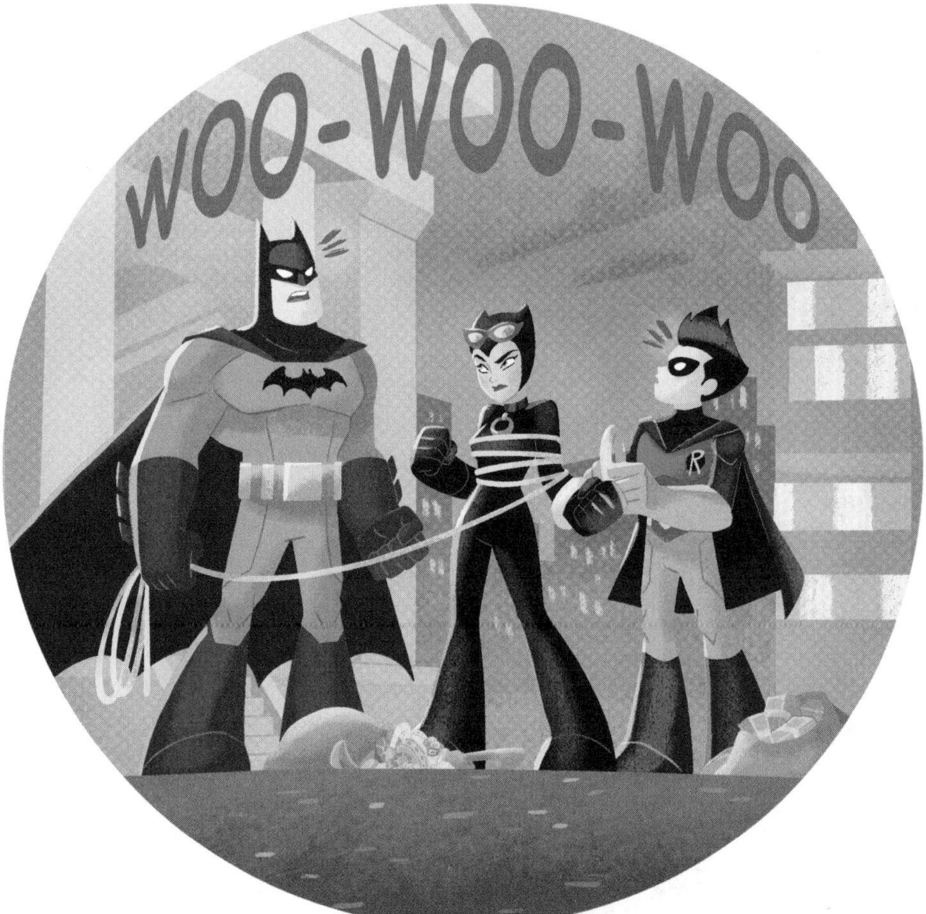
WOO-WOO-WOO

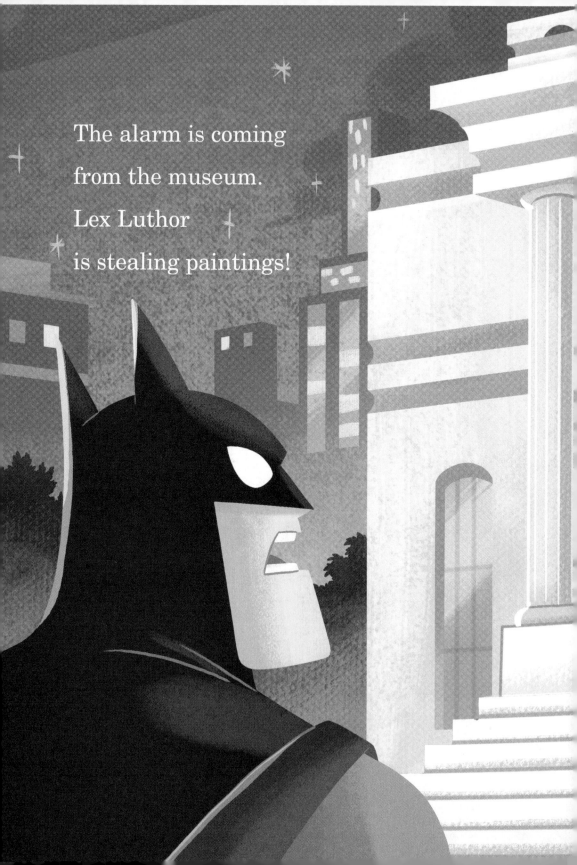

The alarm is coming
from the museum.
Lex Luthor
is stealing paintings!

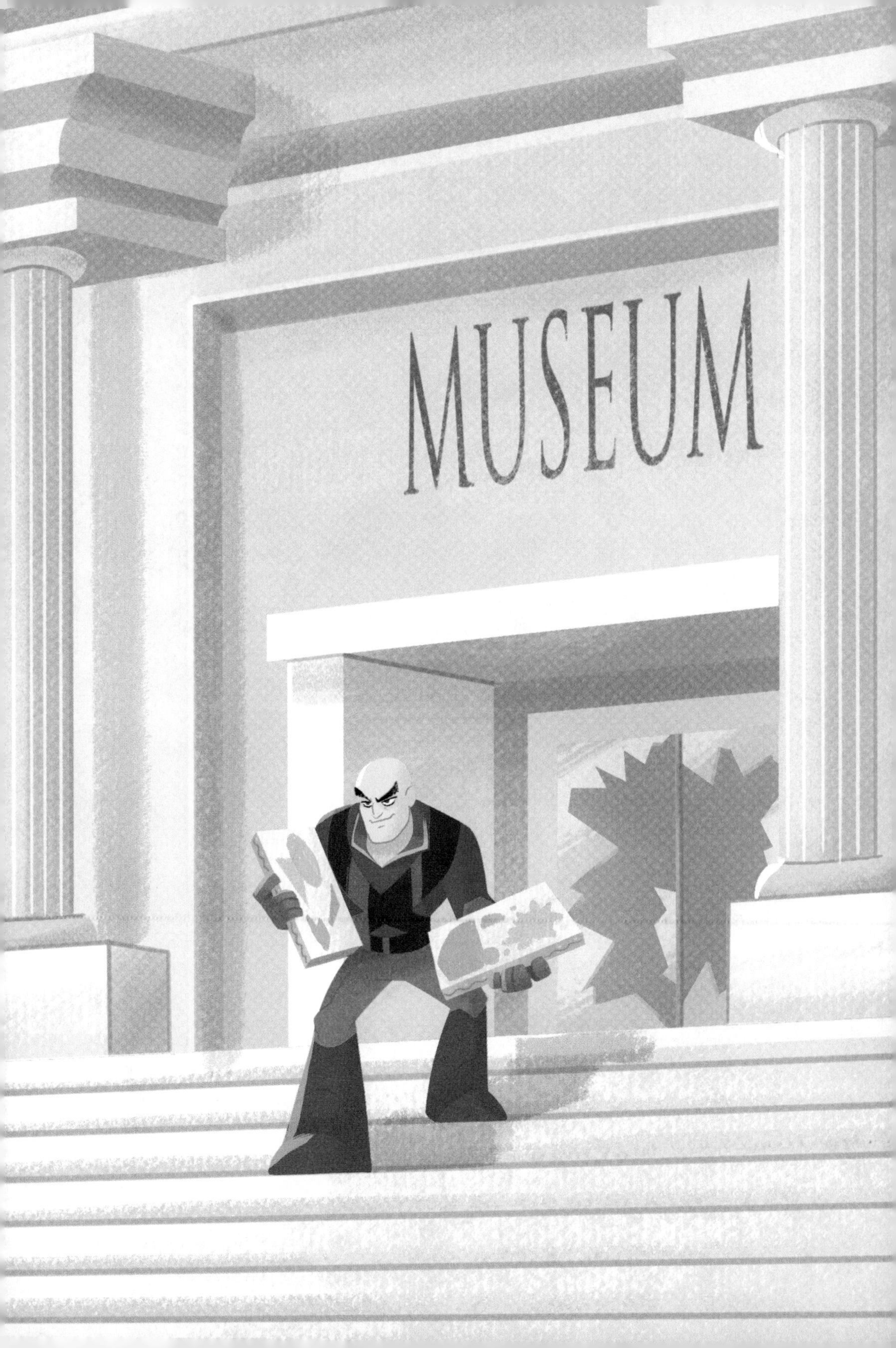
MUSEUM

Catwoman laughs.

Now Batman and Robin

must stop TWO crooks.

Batman will stop Lex Luthor.

Robin will keep an eye on Catwoman.

Two crooks are easy for the two heroes.

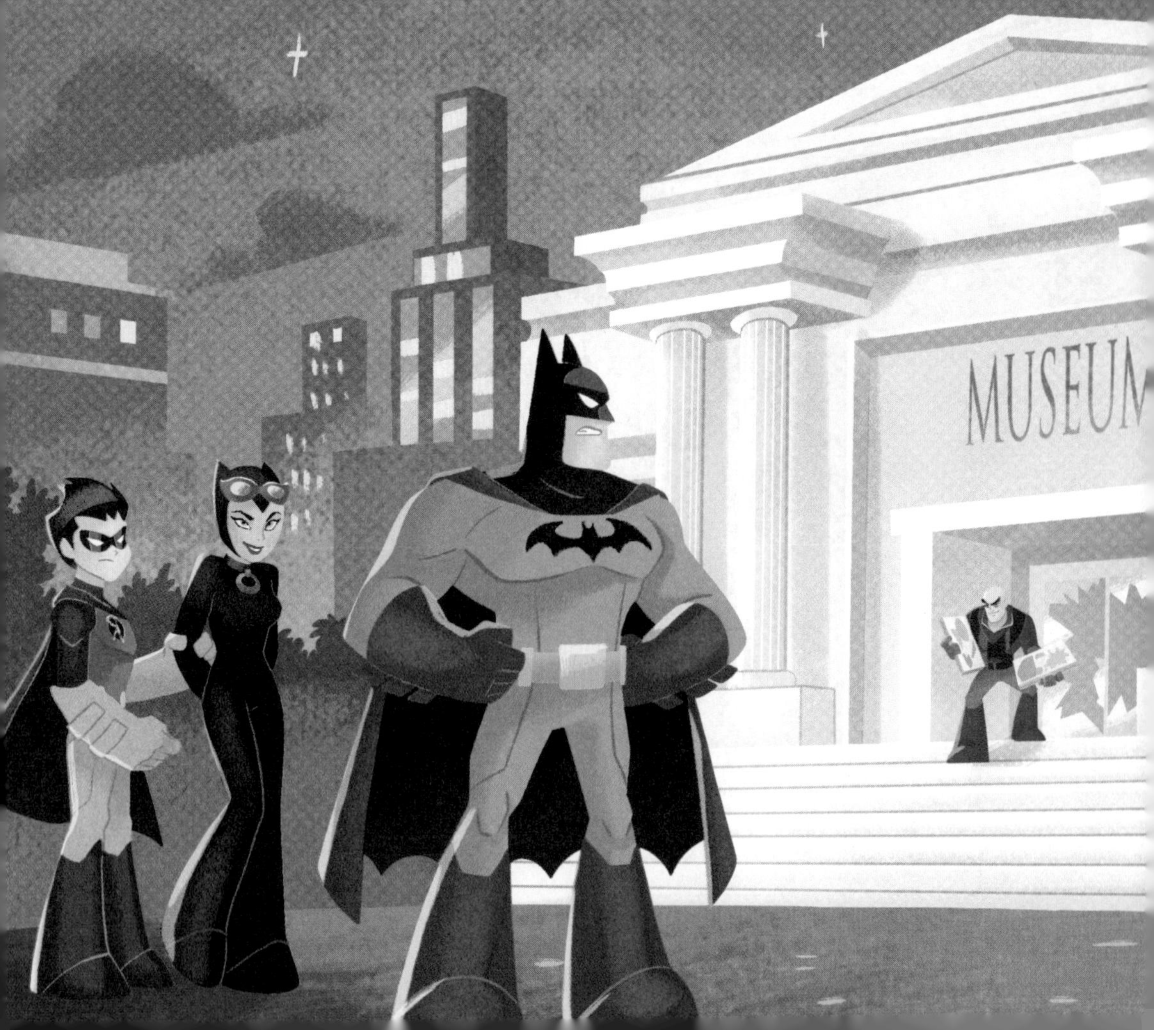
MUSEUM

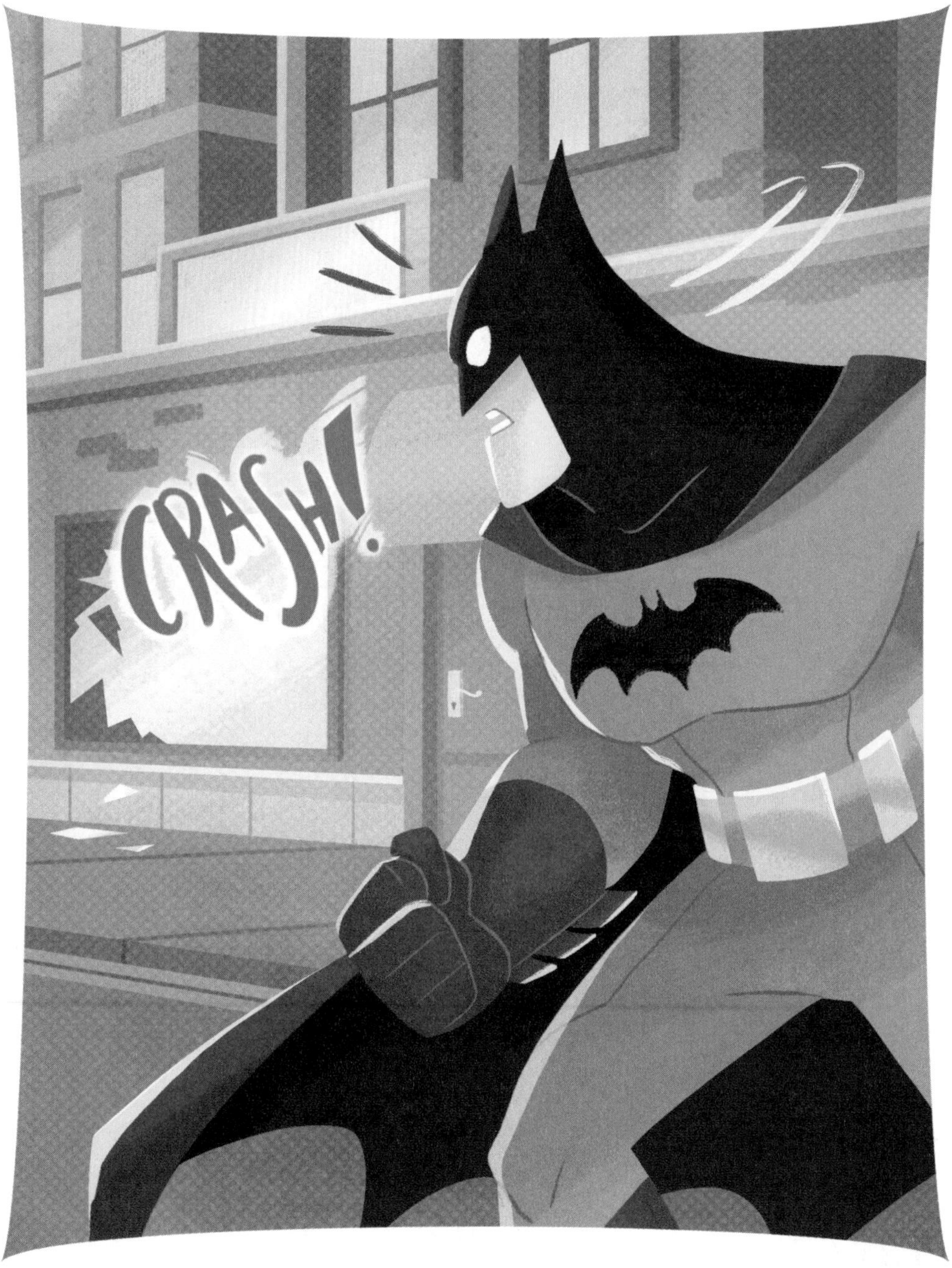
CRASH!

Uh, oh. What is that noise?

Someone is breaking a window!

Oh, no!

Cheetah is robbing

the jewelry store!

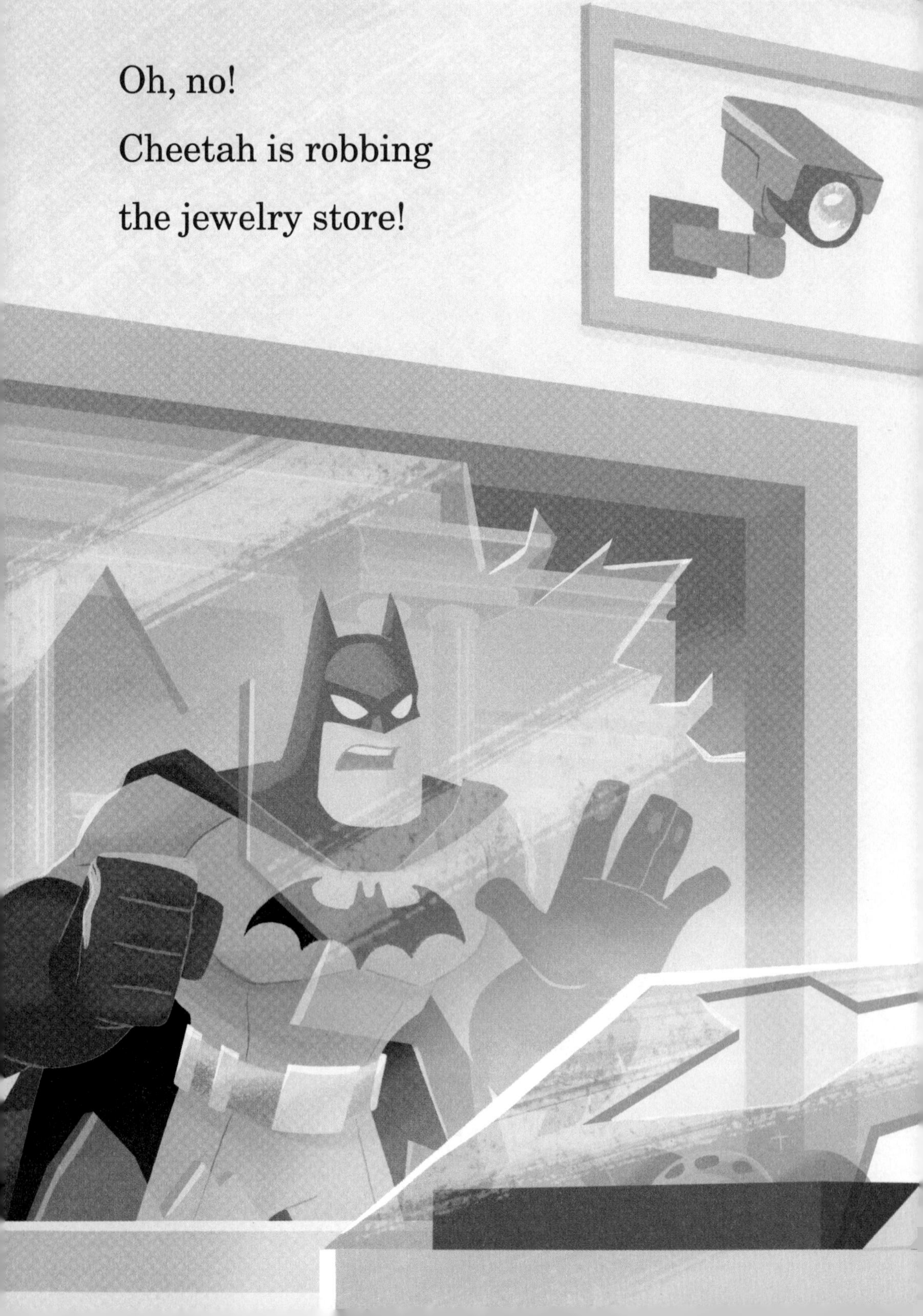

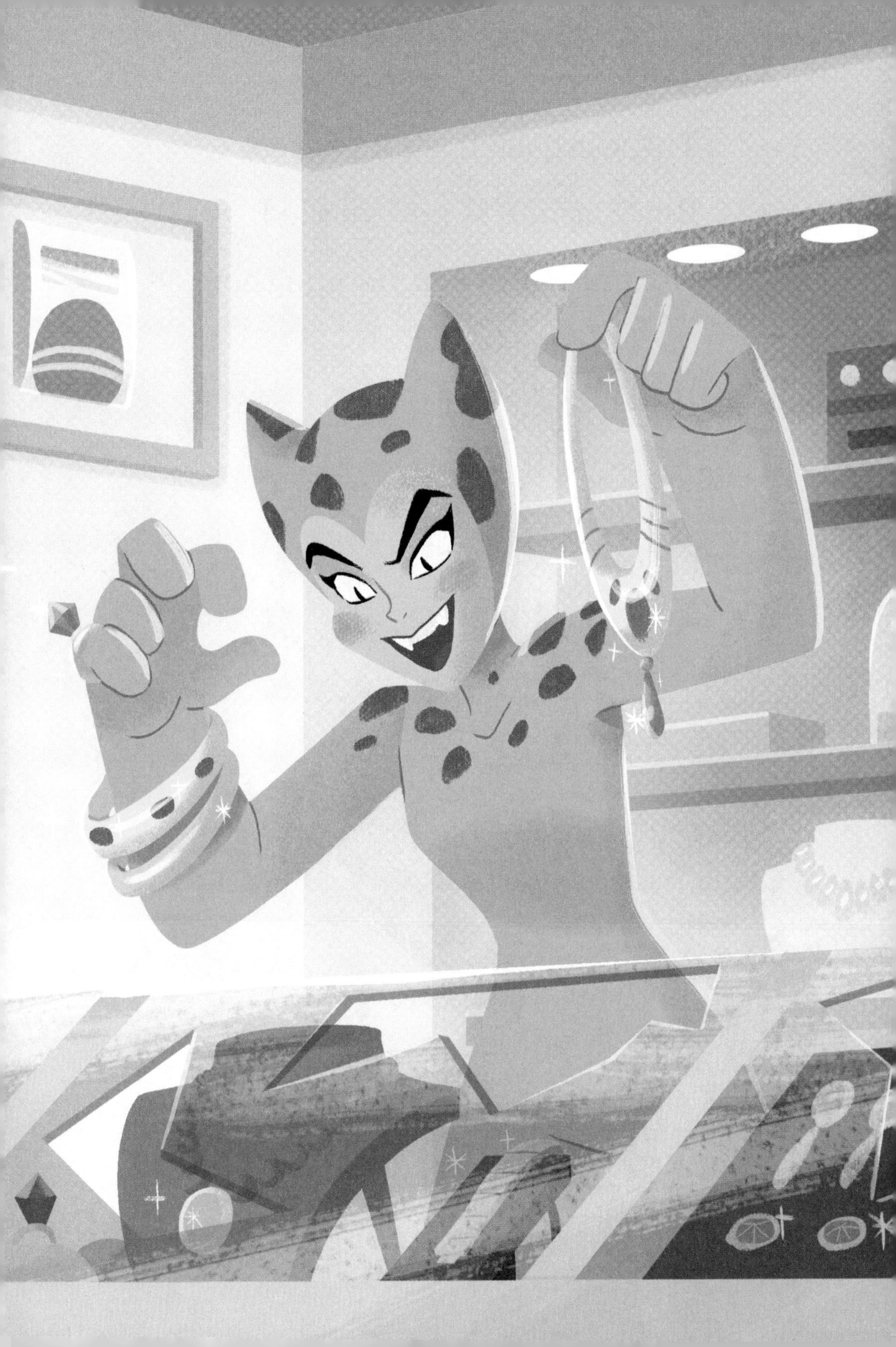

Three crooks is a lot of crooks!

But Batman is not worried.

He and Robin can handle them.

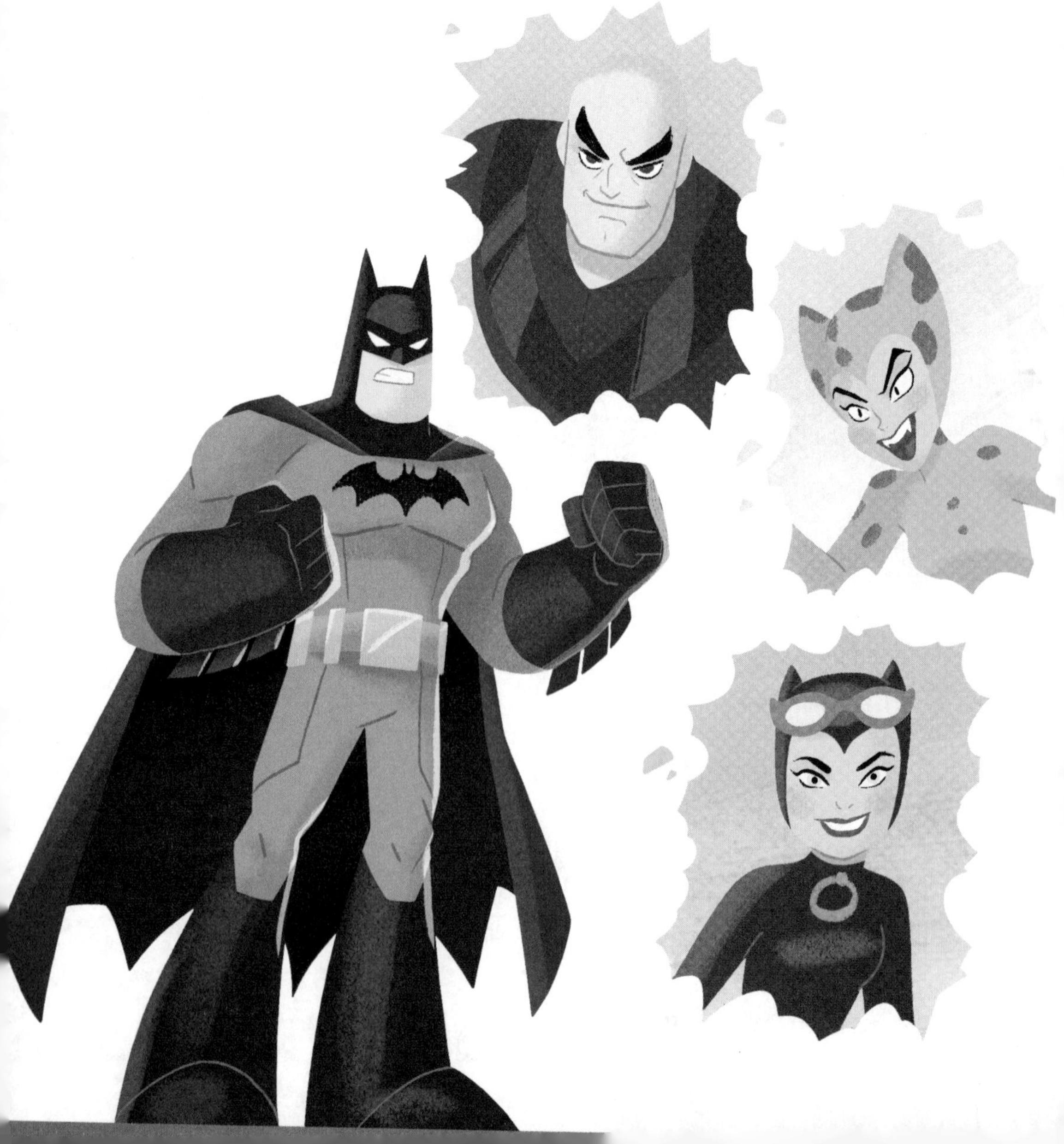

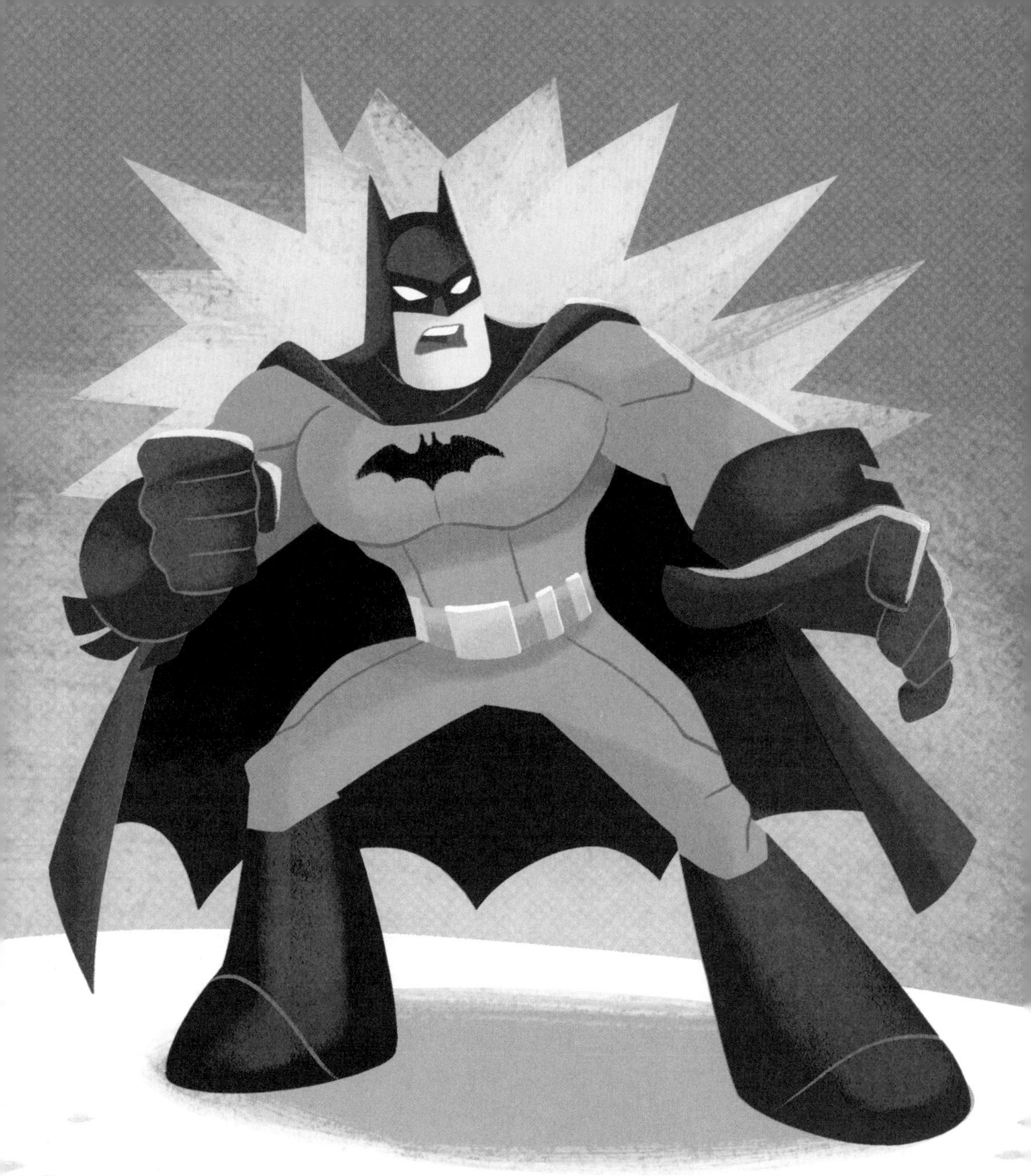

Then Batman hears loud footsteps!

Who could THAT be?

It’s ANOTHER bad guy!
Gorilla Grodd is stealing gold
bars from a big truck!

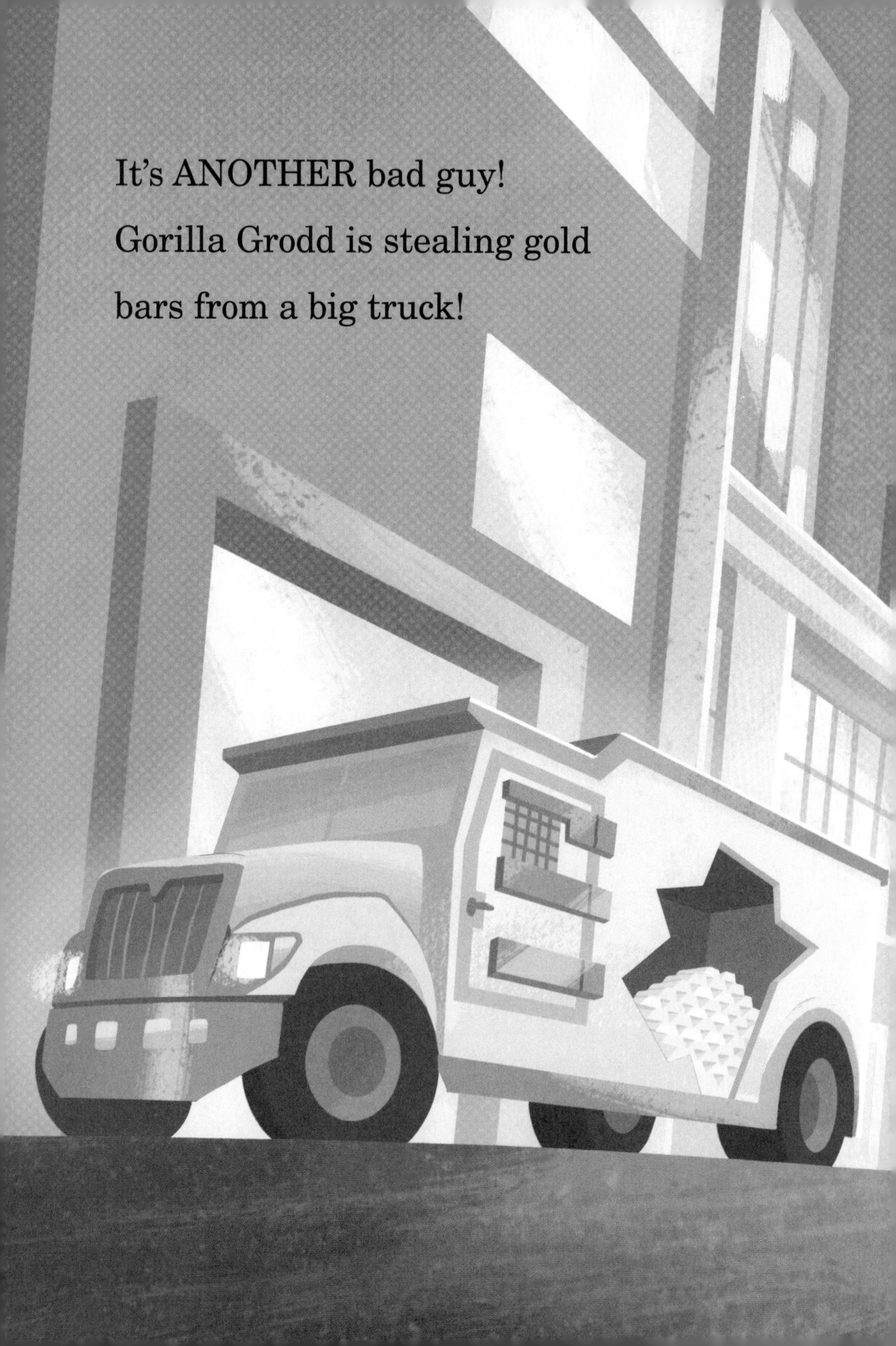

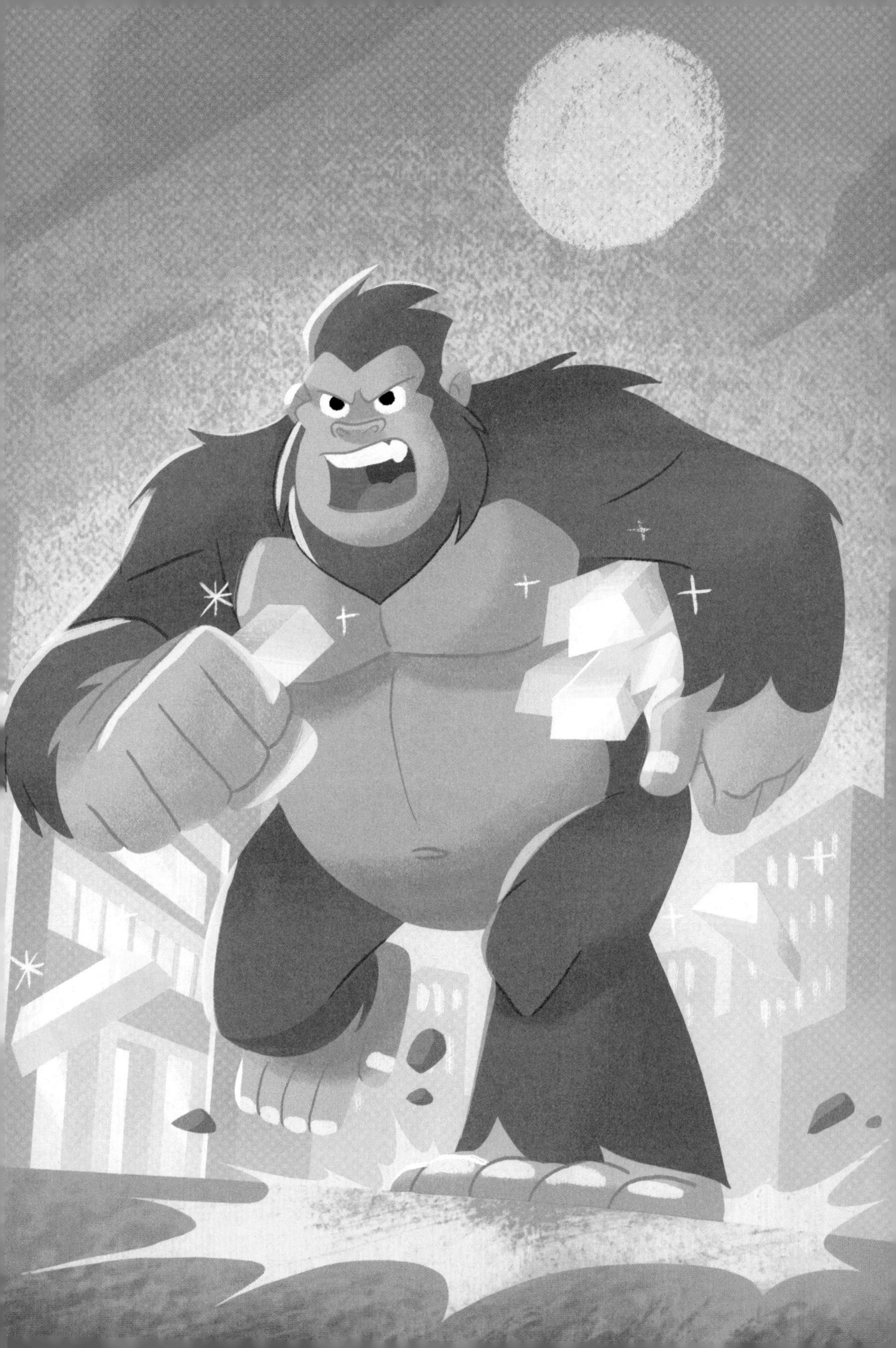

Catwoman smiles.

This was her plan!

"You two can't catch ALL of us," she says.

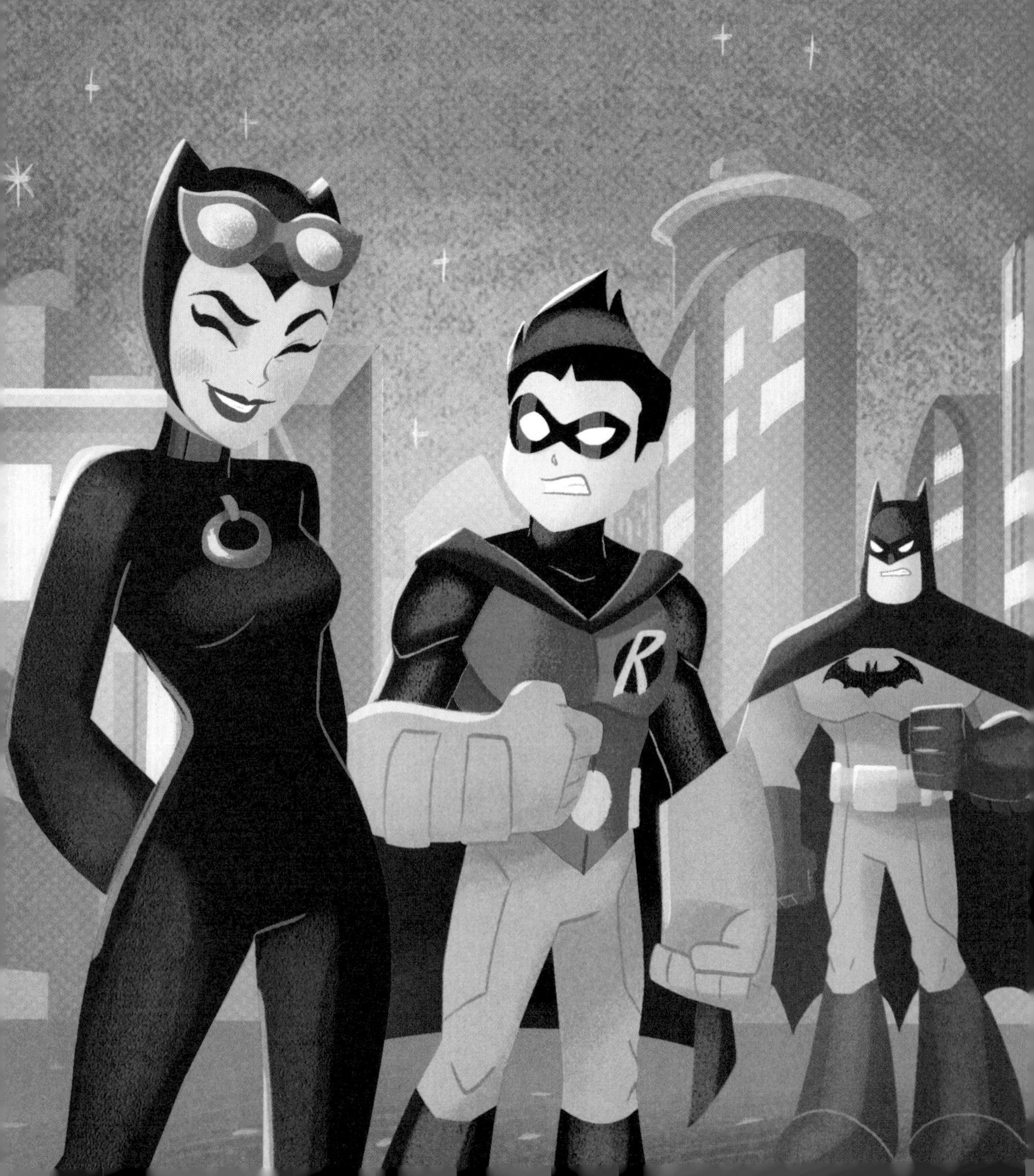

Batman and Robin need help!
Batman presses the button on his belt
to call his friends!

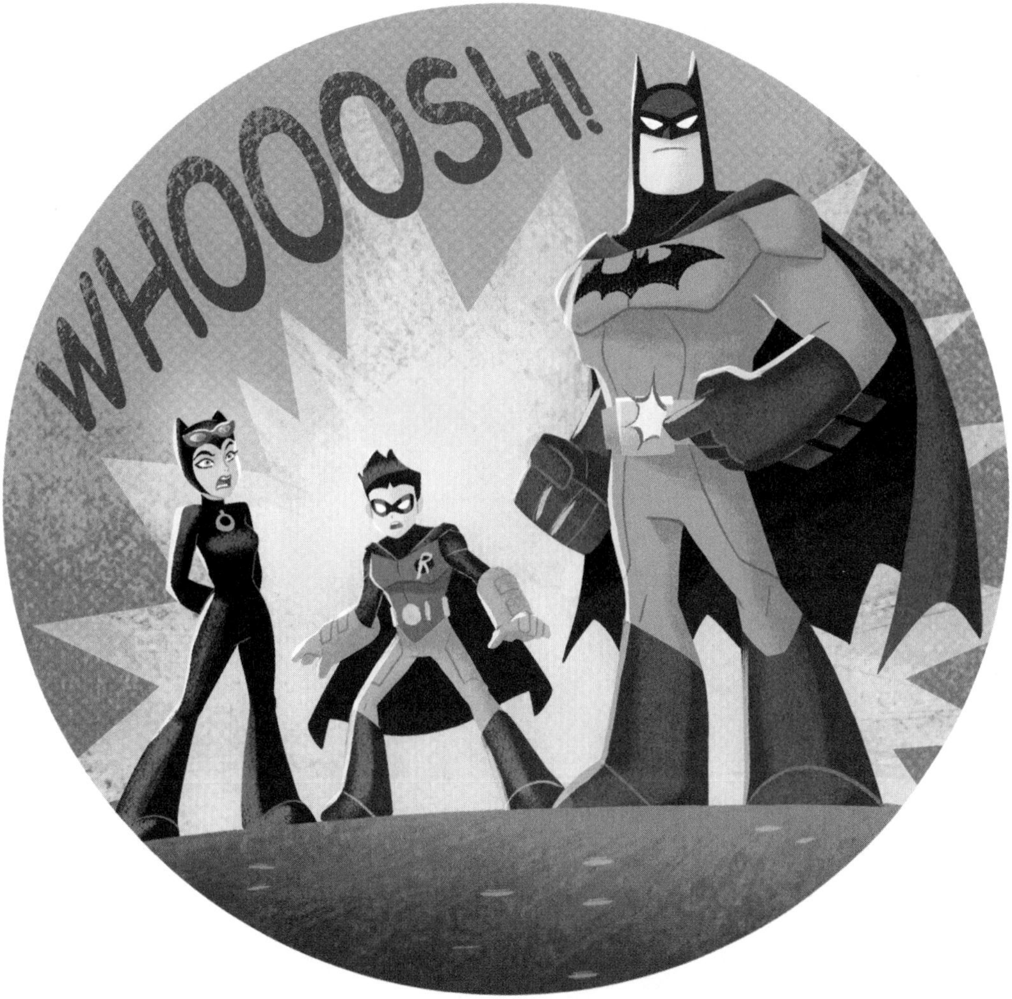
WHOOOSH!

What's that sound?
Is that another villain?

No, it's Superman,

Wonder Woman, and The Flash!

The Super Friends are strong and brave.

These heroes are always ready to help!

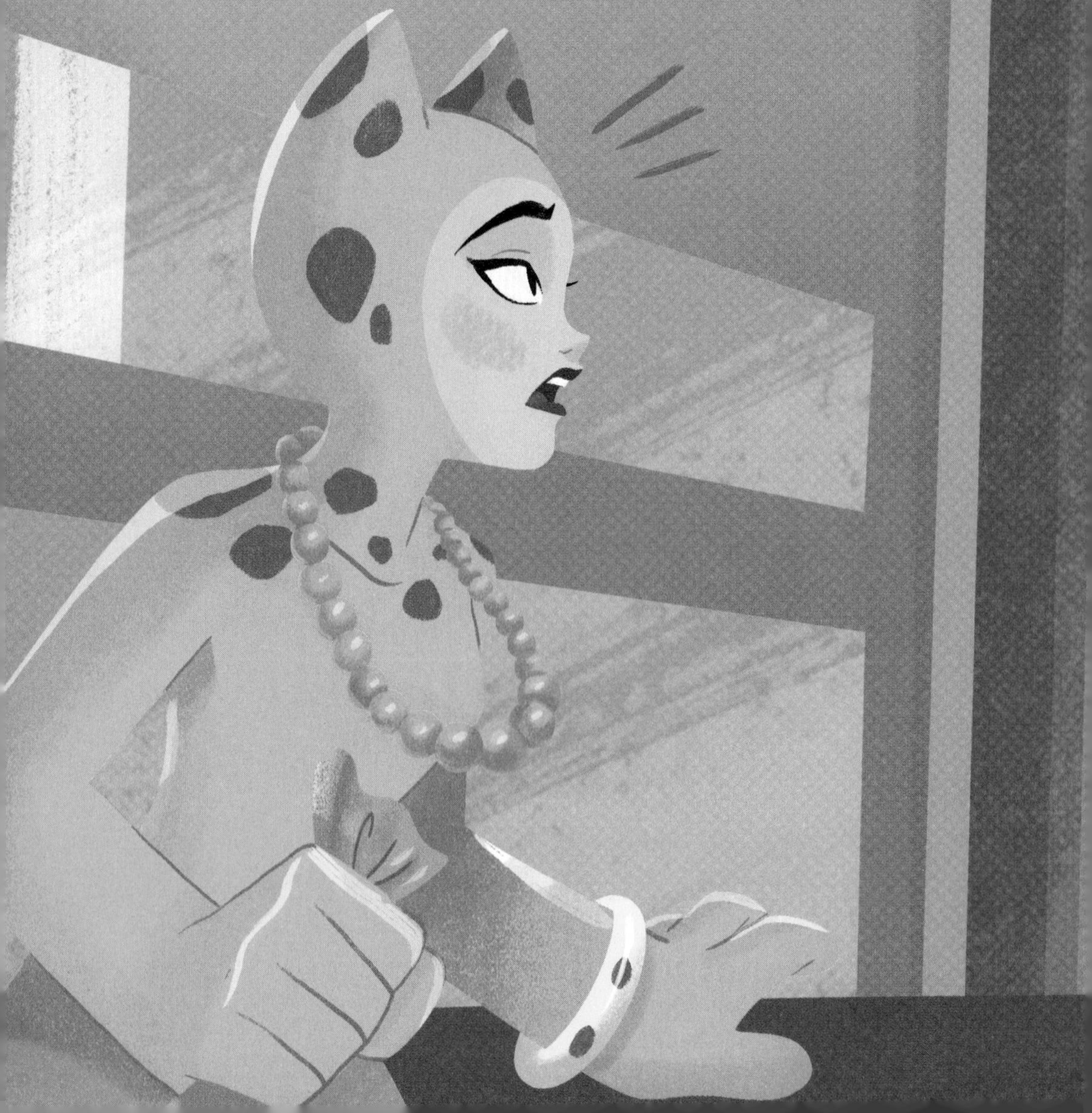

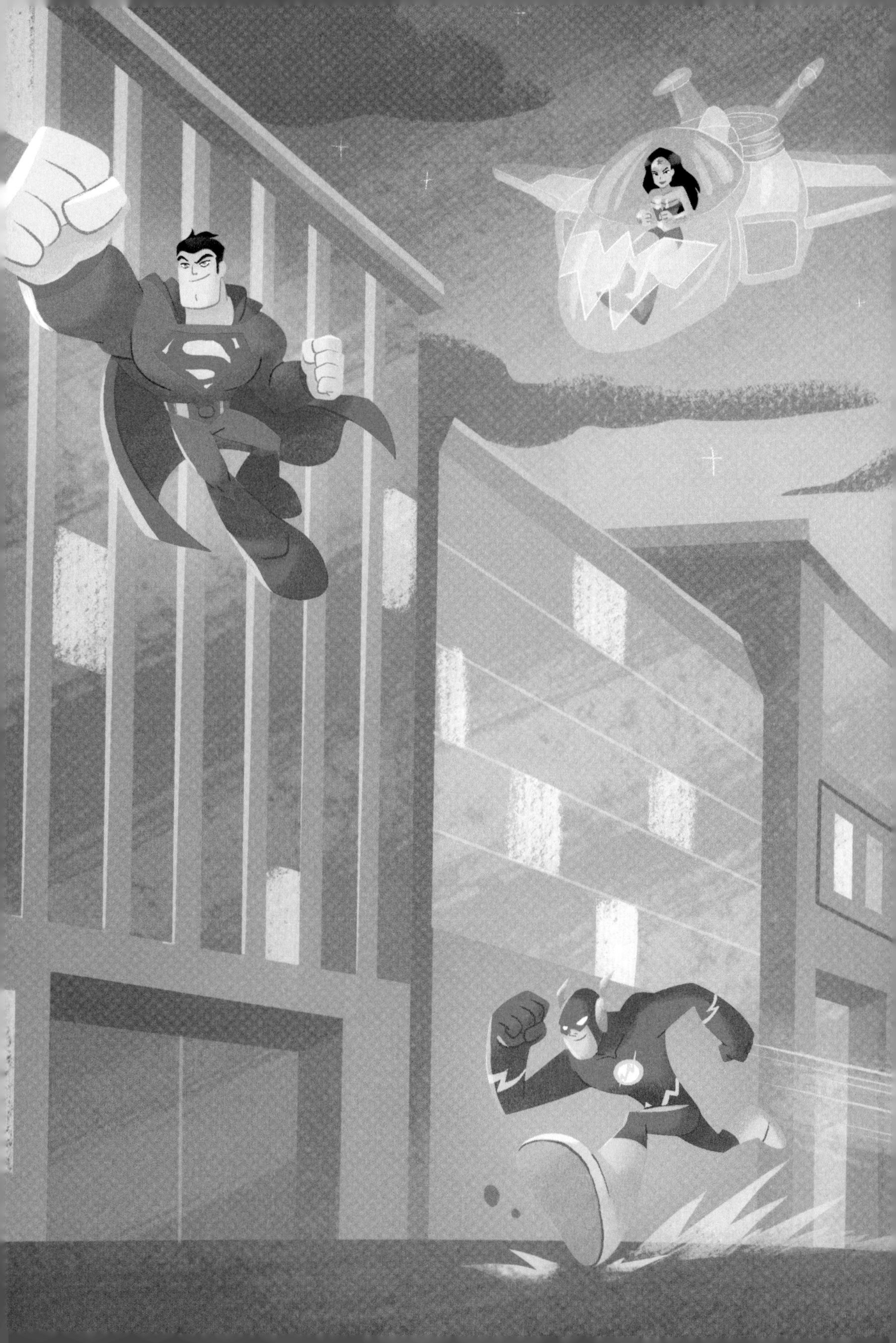

Superman has super-strength
and super-speed.
He captures Lex Luthor and
carries him up into the sky.
Lex Luthor drops the paintings.
Nice try, Lex!

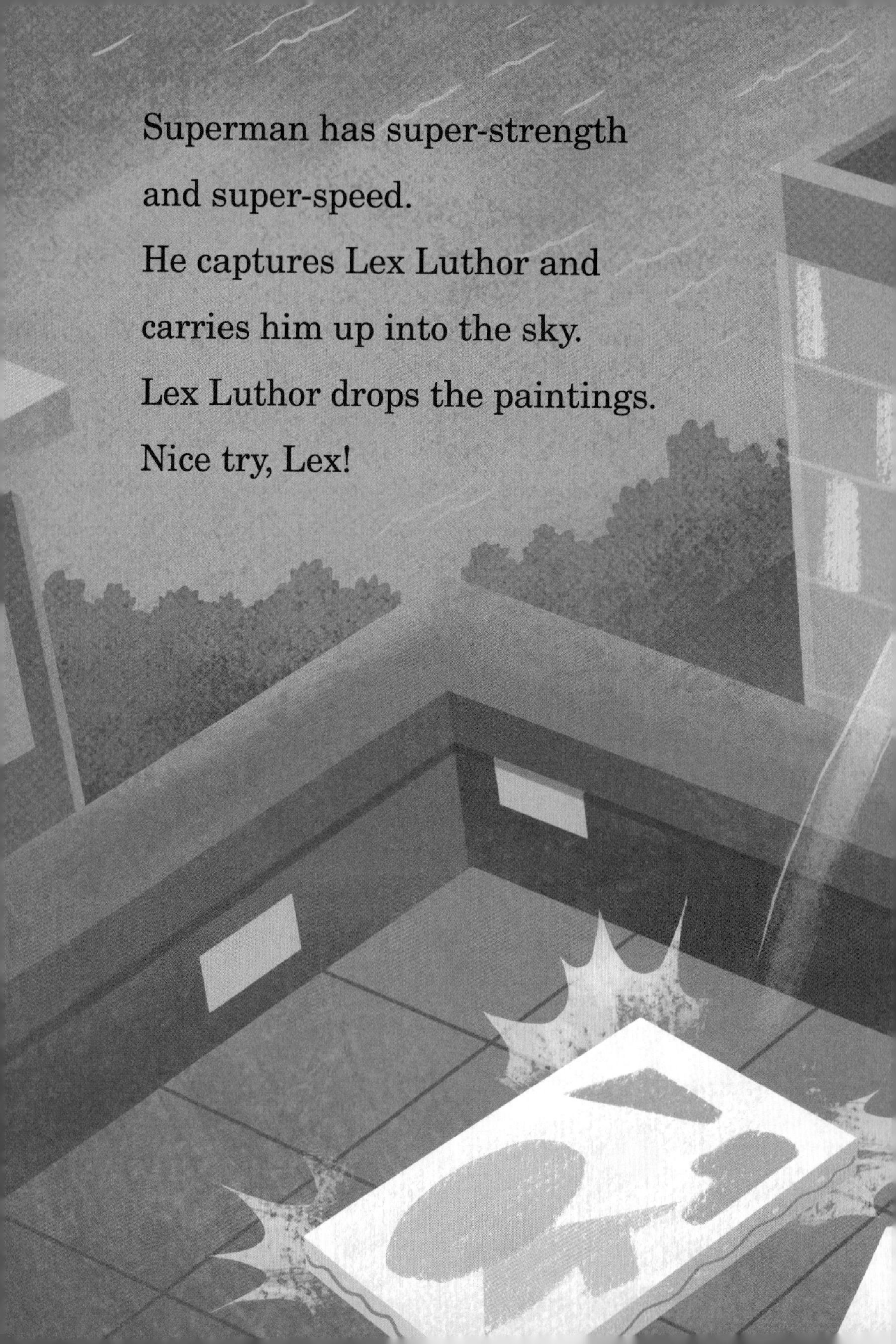

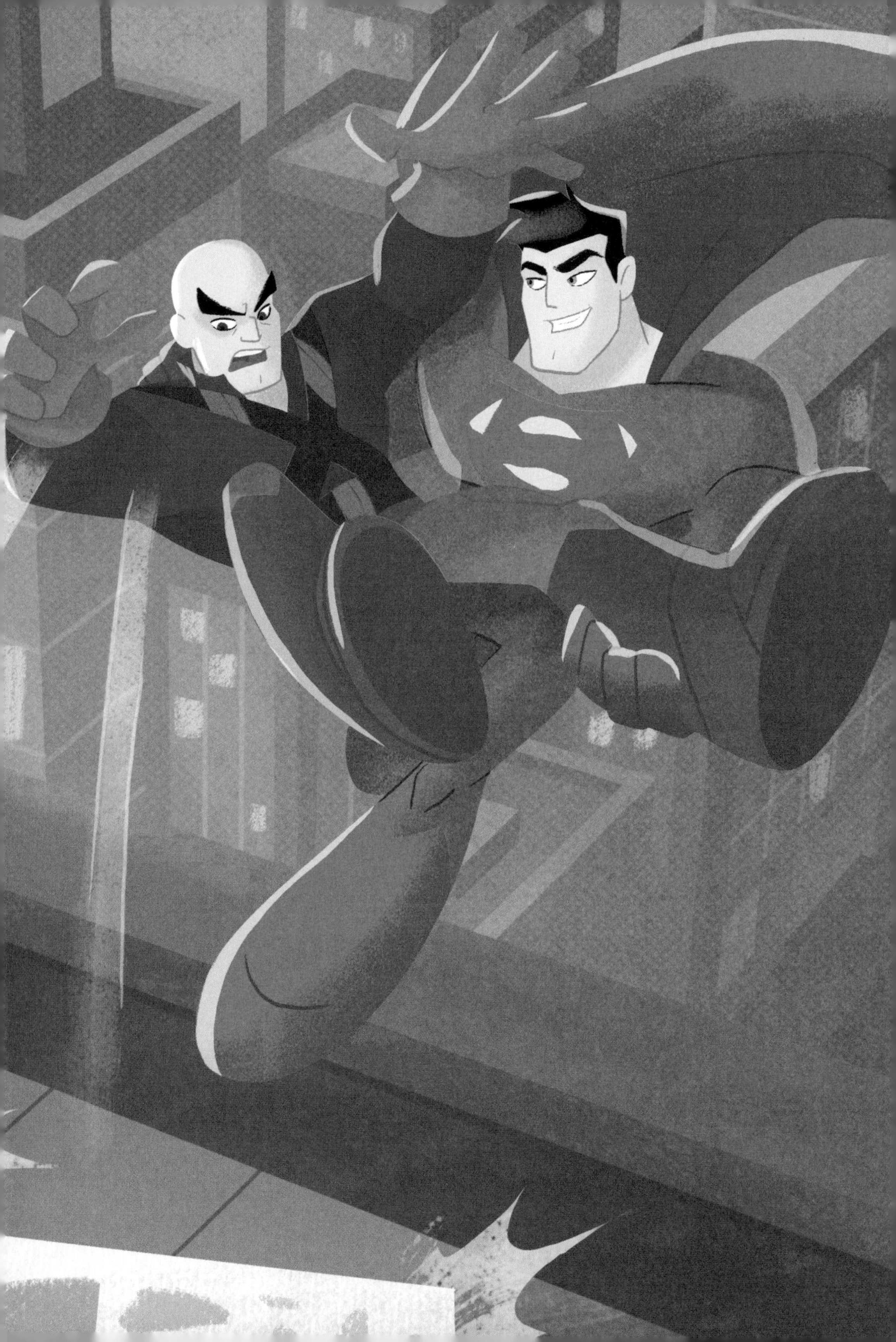

Wonder Woman twirls
her golden Lasso of Truth.
She snags Cheetah
and the stolen jewels.
Sorry, Cheetah!

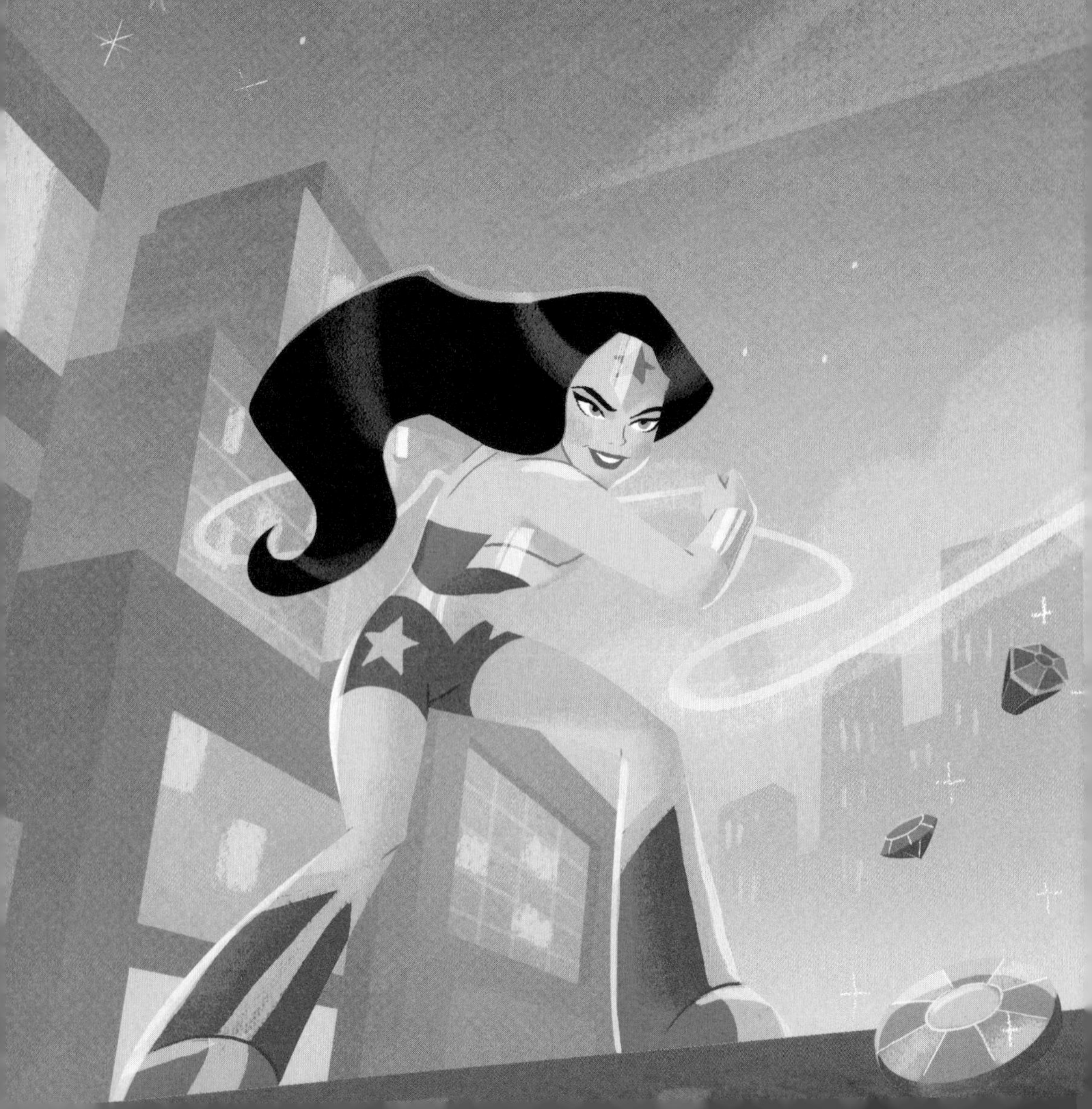

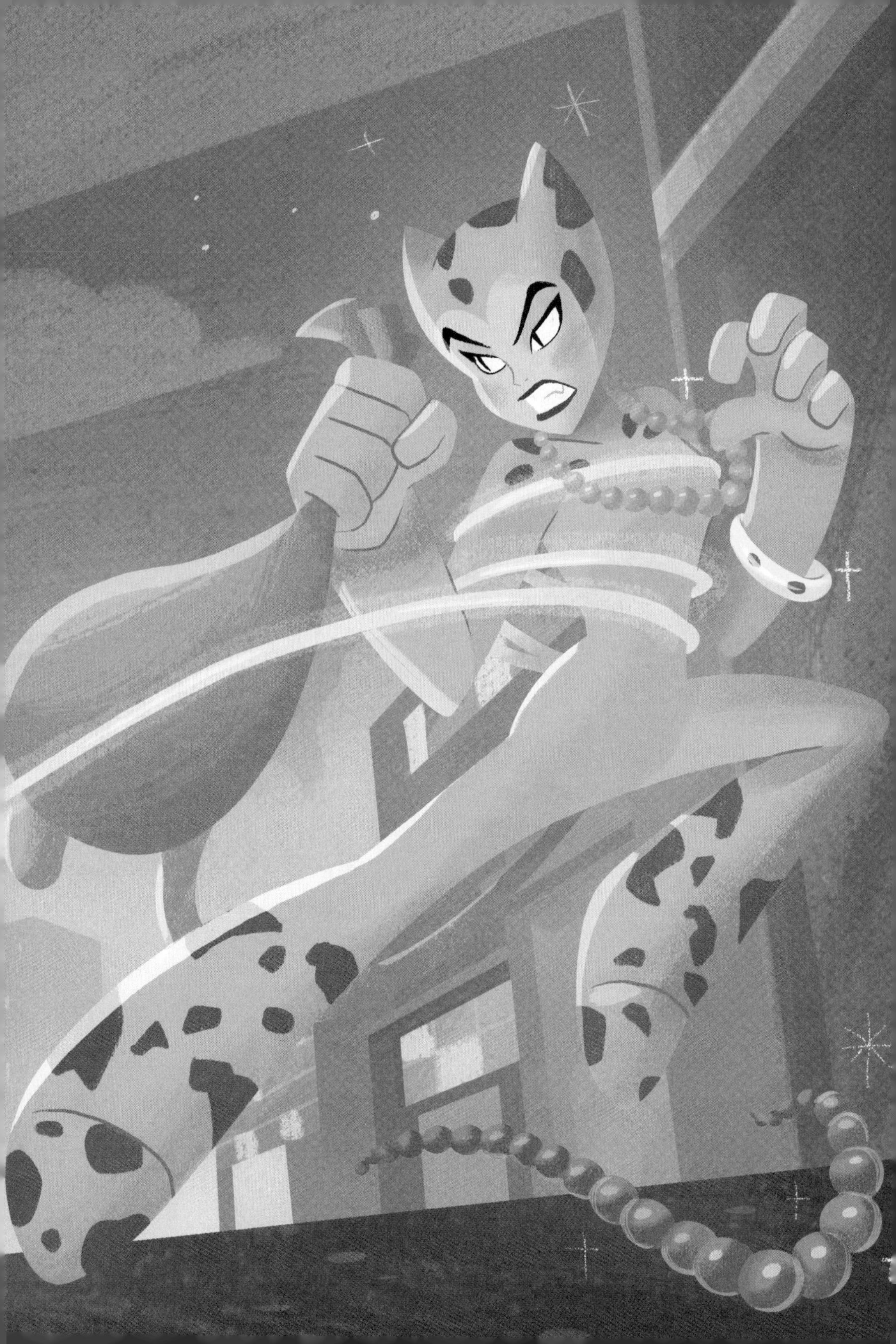

Not so fast, Grodd!
The Flash ties up Gorilla Grodd
at super-speed.

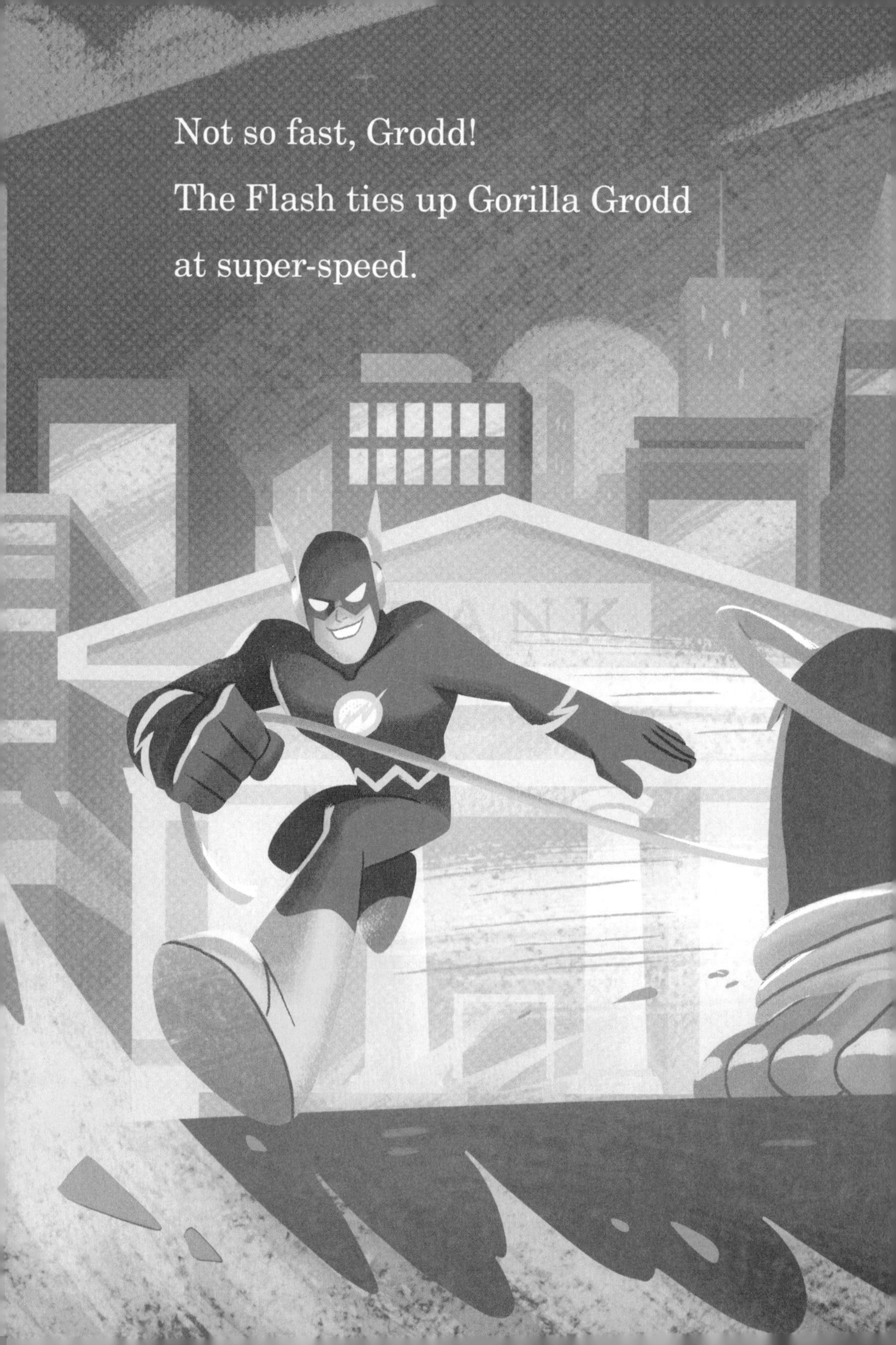

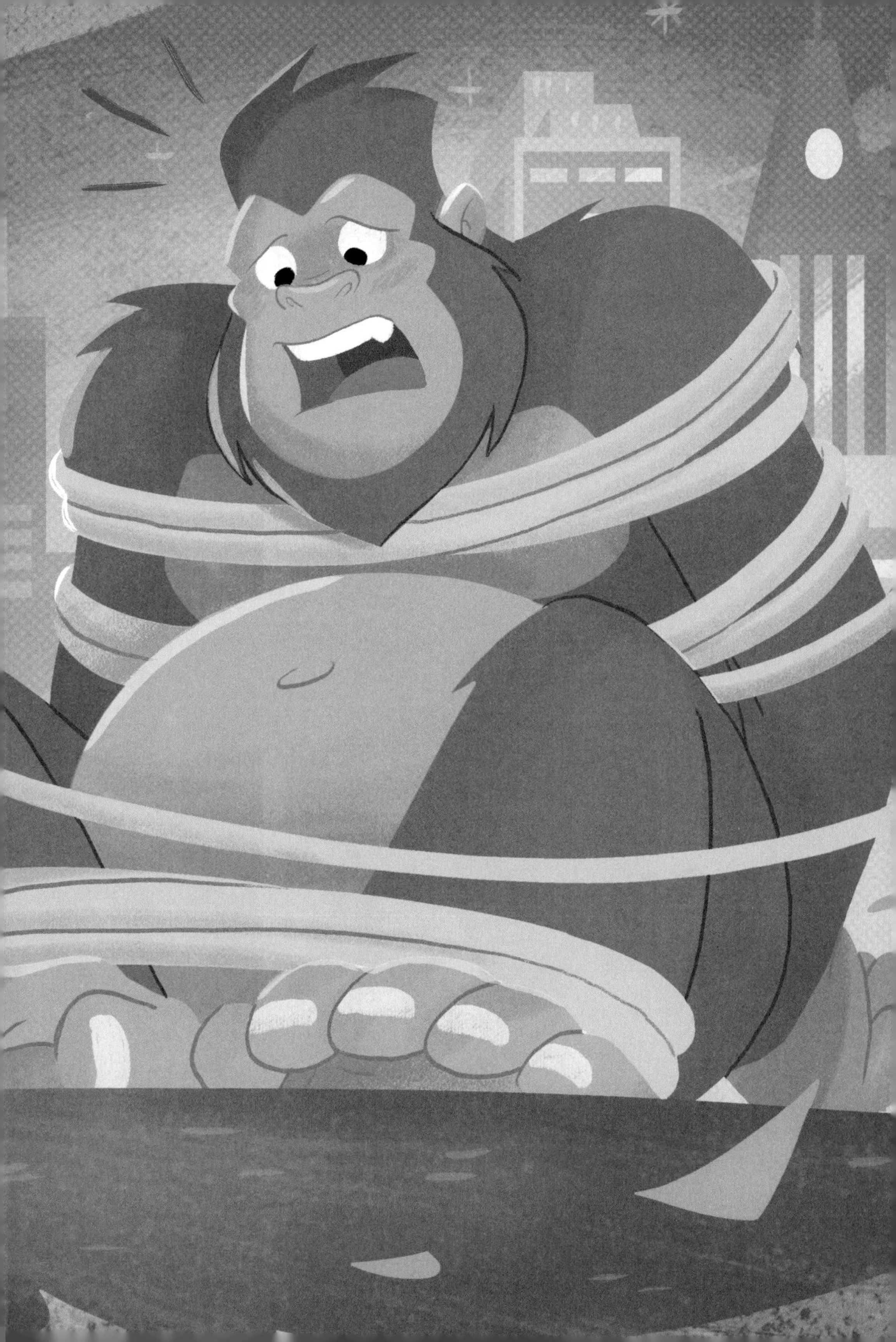

The Super Friends
catch all the crooks.
"Thanks for your help!"
says Batman.

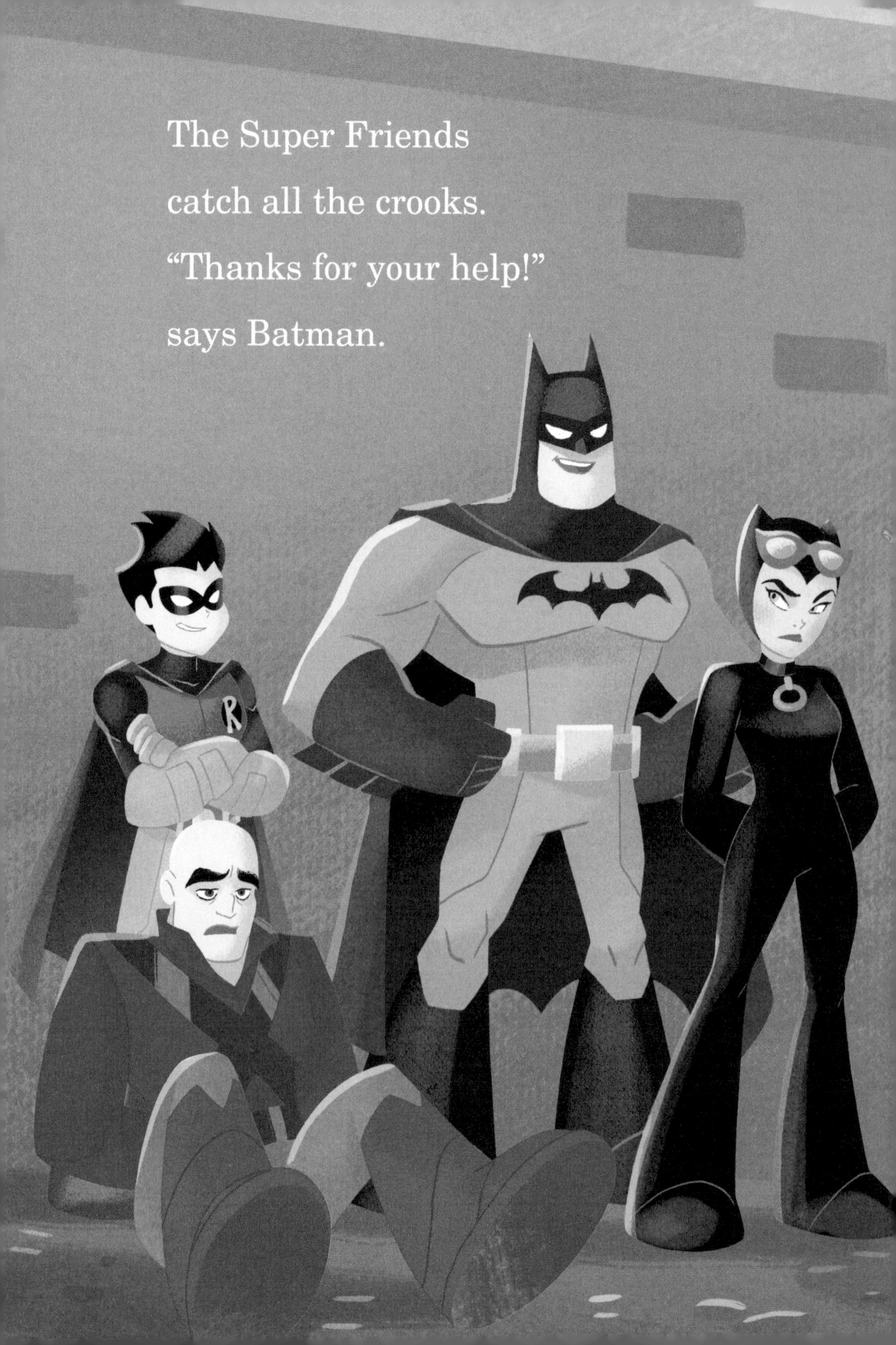

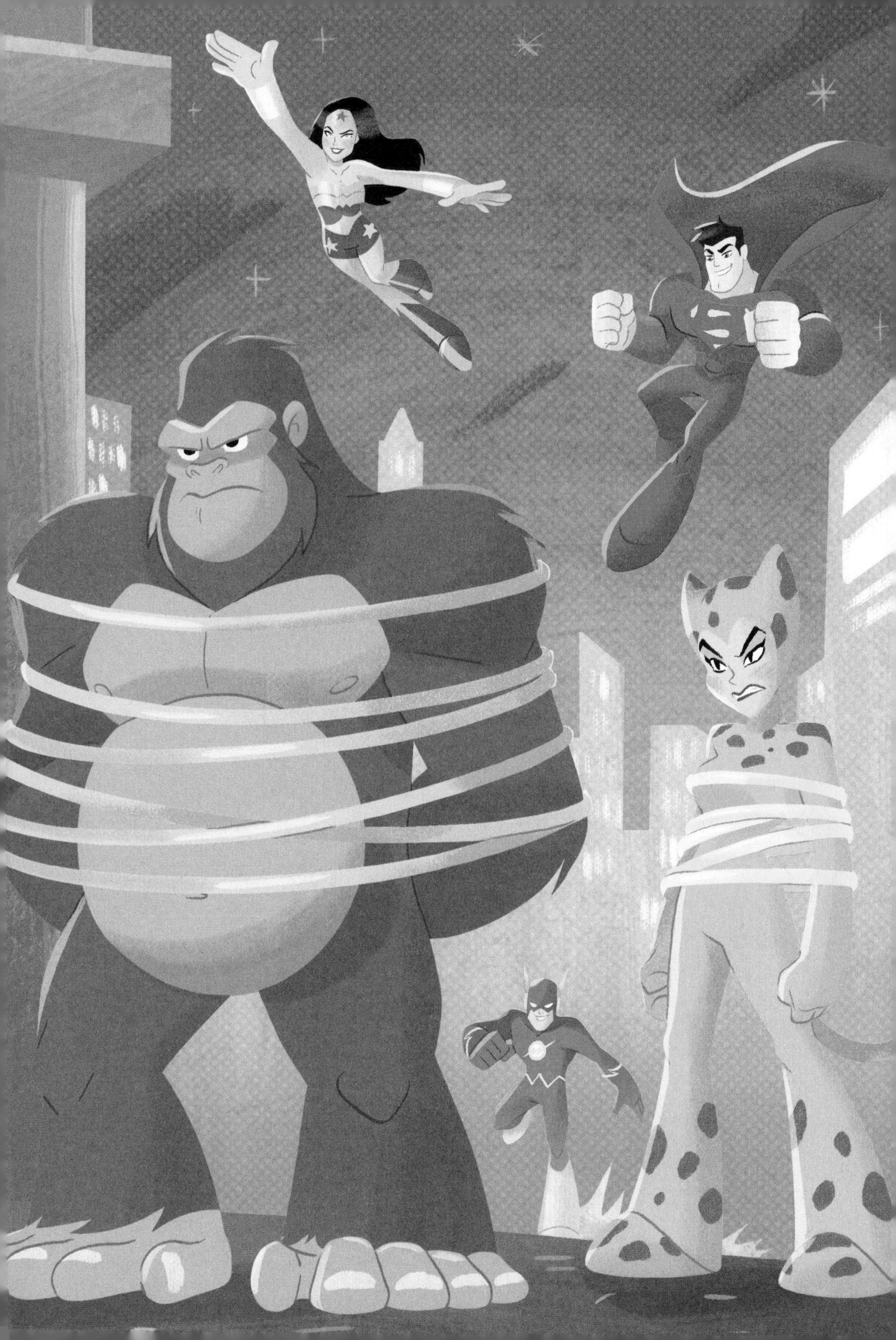

The crooks are
going to jail.
Gotham City is safe again.
Good job, Batman!
Thanks, Super Friends!

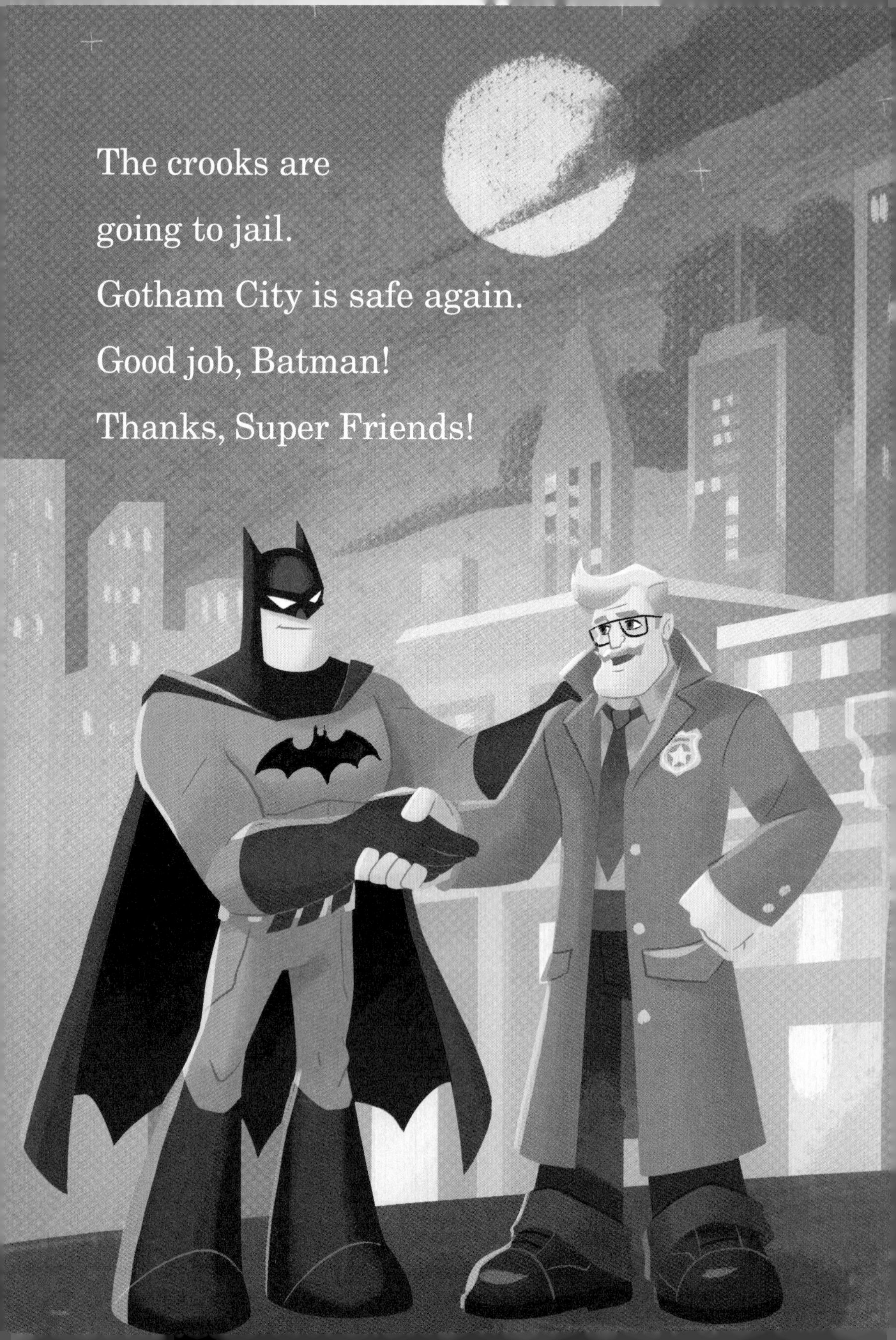

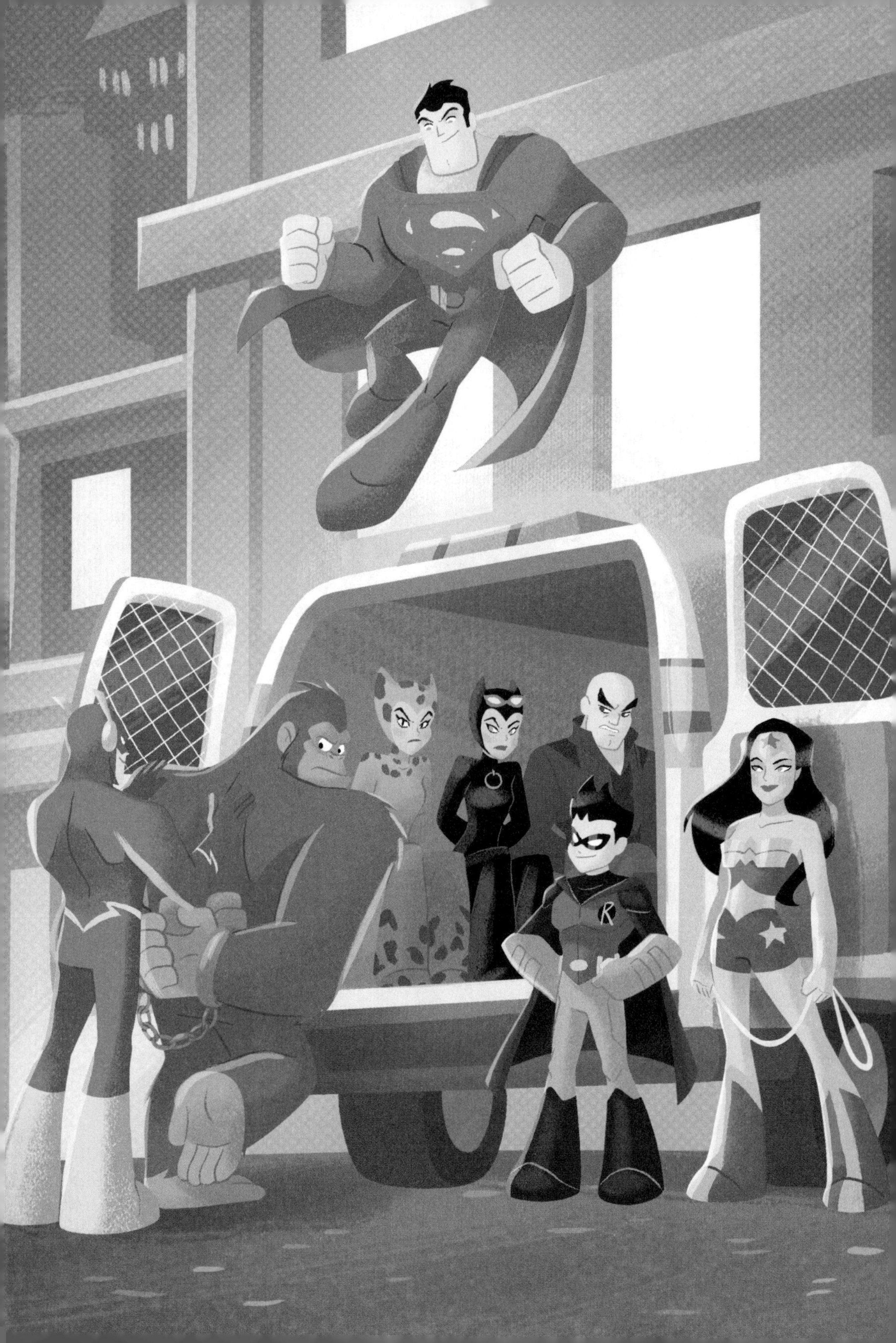

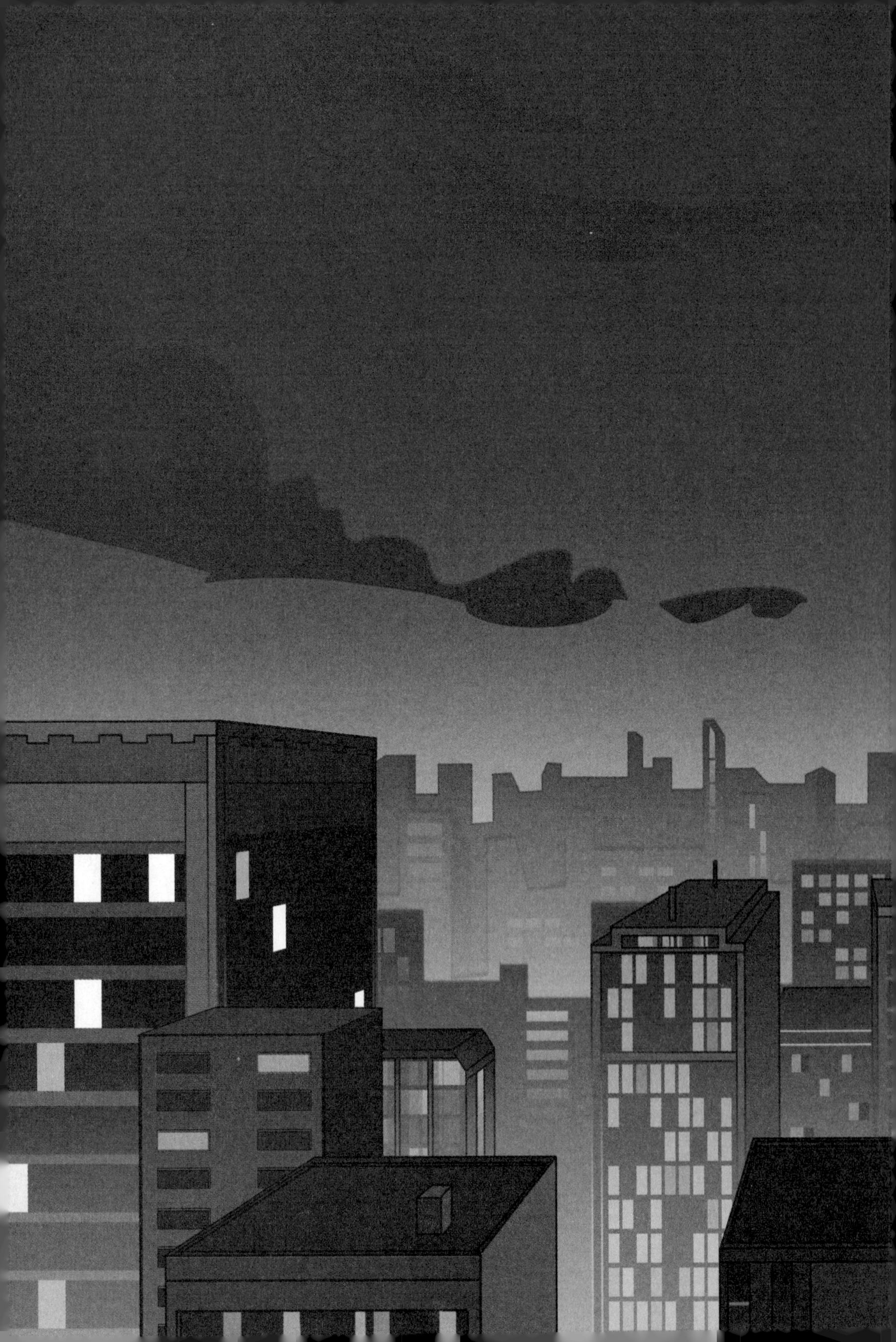